FLAMINGO

DESIRES

a mystery

REVISED
VERSION

by

Edward Eriksson

CHAPTER ONE
Fall from Grace

It was one of those casual dramas that start off breezily and end in grimness.

Tom Flynn had smiled at his secretary, passing her desk at nine-forty-five holding a large cup of black coffee. He pushed through the door of his County Legislator's office, clicking it carefully behind him. After placing the coffee on the edge of his desk, he went to his private lavatory to check himself in the mirror. Washing his hands, he saw his pleasant, clean-shaven face, his witty blue eyes (looking a little tired) and his blue-and-yellow striped tie knotted neatly under the collar of his white shirt. He straightened the lapels of his dark blue blazer, nodded approval, then went and sat at his desk. He called his secretary on the intercom and, as if by afterthought, asked her to go and get him a plain bagel with cream cheese. Then he surveyed the paperwork Melissa had laid out for him. He smiled ironically on the right side of his mouth before taking a clean sheet of paper and drawing three large dollar signs on it. Then he opened his desk drawer to remove a silver .22 Luger. He gazed deliberately towards the door of his office. Taking a deep breath, he pointed the pistol at a spot below his right ear and pulled the trigger.

That's how Laureen Metcalf, recreated the scene in her mind; she, the *Newsday* reporter who knew Flynn well and who wrote the articles that apparently caused him to shoot himself.

"Suicide," was the simple sentiment of Henry Stallard, the County Attorney.

A week earlier, one day before Election Day, she, this *Newsday* reporter, Laureen Metcalf, published the last of four articles that exposed a cadre of politicians who, among other offenses, managed to steal seventeen million dollars from the Suffolk County treasury. This cadre included Tom Flynn, who lost his bid for re-election and looked forward to an indictment for embezzlement of public funds. Some friends of Flynn's offered the information that the dead man had checked into a motel on Route 347 an hour after the balloting counts showed that he would lose. Reports from the motel staff indicated he'd been drinking heavily for the next five days, when he finally presented himself in his office on Monday morning all cleaned up.

The scene of Tom Flynn's waltzing into his office and committing suicide was an imaginative piece of sensational journalism Laureen would never write up, an expression of her horror once she arrived at the scene and understood what had happened. How could it have happened any other way?

She'd collected the details from the police and then from Melissa, who told her of the bagel she brought her boss on a paper plate and found him shortly before ten-thirty. Flynn lay slumped over his desk, his arm dangling, the silver weapon on the floor, his cheek resting on the paper with three dollar signs on it, and the coffee container undisturbed at the far corner of the desk. Obviously suicide: but there were no witnesses, no note, only dollar signs, and no corroboration in the neatness of Flynn's attire, unless to avoid suspicion as he entered the office. The desk drawer was partially open, a place where Laureen supposed that Flynn had kept the gun.

Laureen saw horror everywhere, especially in the picture of Flynn's suavity in committing the act. She'd been a friend of his and, more intimately, a friend of his wife's, of Sandra's. They were emotional, lively people. She didn't see ahead when she began her research how deeply Flynn was involved. *County Crooks Steal $17 Million!* That, on the eve of Election Day, was the headline.

She wondered how she could've handled the man more discreetly. Even so, he was a politician and should've been hardened to the ebb and flow of political fortunes. Outwardly, he was a pretty chipper guy. All the more to regret. She'd seen towards the end where it was all going, disaster looming in the atmosphere. Given the momentum, there was no chance of rescue.

There was, of course, the chance that he didn't kill himself; that in some way would let her off the hook. Maybe Stallard was wrong. Still, that gun in Flynn's office.

The day the suicide hit the news room, word went around that she was the one who drove Flynn to it. She heard the whispers, the jokes, too, and while she tried to believe the comments weren't racial--she'd become the prominent black reporter on the paper--she thought of getting away, anywhere, Mexico, Costa Rica. She'd done her job, and this death was her reward. Get away, far away: the phrase kept passing through her head. Without her husband, though, without Rodger, she'd be desolate; and there was no way he could take a break in the middle of the semester. He could skip out for a week; but she knew he wouldn't, he the straight-arrow professor at Peconic College. It seemed she'd entered a play as a character--caught in a plot and acting out a part. Now those spasms of guilt told her that something else had to come out of this, something she couldn't get away from, something destined particularly for her.

There was the final article to write. There was the morgue to visit, as next day she went alone to see the corpse of Tom Flynn in Hauppauge. Afterwards she couldn't speak of the visit to anyone.

She spent the following days in self-torture, agonizing over her articles again and again, and then the facts of Flynn's embezzlement and the details of his death. There would be more, she told herself; and that "more" promised no relief.

Now, a week later, on another Monday, she found herself in a ghoulish mob scene. It happened to be her birthday, but she was in no mood to celebrate. It was another act in the drama, but here she waited in the wings. She stood whispering notes into her I-phone as she stood at the edge of the funeral crowd--a crowd that jammed up traffic for several hundred yards on Setauket's Main Street. She wouldn't have been there, but her editor, Joe Fallon, had insisted. He also flattered her with the notion that she'd be considered for a Pulitzer Prize, adding that she ought to finish what she'd begun. She didn't offer any fuss; she told herself that this is what she deserved. But she hung back in the outer mass, not wanting to be caught on news film or in any way seen hovering like a scandal-sheet vulture. Even in the rear of the crush, she was tall enough to see over the heads of those down front. Now all eyes were turned to the church steps. Soon all tongues were silent.

From her distance she saw the scene in a regretful blur. The November sky, grayish-brown in its smooth cloud-cover, cast an amber light on the occasion, covering it in a nostalgic aura, like that of an old, fading photograph. Only the men in their black hats and overcoats stood out, fussing about the casket at the church door and giving directions to one another. And there was Frank Van Dam, the six-footer with his fluttery shock of reddish-brown hair, catching her eye and nodding. Amazed that he could pick her out at this distance, she nodded back, almost against her will. Some of the others there, three of them, would soon be under indictment, but not Mr. Van Dam, the young party leader, a.k.a. the Boy Wonder, the one she sensed was guilty of manipulating the others, but someone no evidence pointed to. Part of the reason, she suspected, was that he was her secret informer, the source of many an obscure fact that doomed the others. Indeed, she would have been lost without inside access to all the slippery business of the ruling party. Still, for Van Dam to inform on the others made no sense. Didn't he want his party to win the election?

The funeral had the air of a somber festivity. A bagpipe ensemble of off-duty cops in blue plaid kilts and feathered tam-o-shanters droned mournfully as the casket eased forward, carried by Flynn's political cohorts, and rocked uncertainly down the steps. With the help of the chauffeur, the pallbearers managed to get it into the rear of a black limousine. The politicos were all dressed in black, all wore black fedoras, all except the reddish-haired Frank Van Dam, and all seemed pale as their shirts. The dead man had been a popular figure, elected three times to the County

Legislature. While no one was glad that he'd died, the grandeur of the funeral offered the impression that the sorry business was done and that Tom Flynn, dying for the sins of many, could now be laid to rest. The judgment of suicide was slurred over so that he might have a Catholic mass. And now, as the bagpipes groaned a rendition of "Amazing Grace," Laureen brought the collar of her black overcoat up around her chin and let her eyelids fall halfway over her eyes, paying a quiet tribute to the man her words had doomed.

She caught herself staring at Van Dam. They'd known each other since high school, twenty years back. They'd even dated, sort of, for a short while. She never trusted him afterwards; but periodically he would bring himself to her attention with a certain look in his eye that made her uncomfortable--and for which, strangely enough, she blamed herself. Hell, he'd been married for twelve years now. Of course, she used the information she'd gotten anonymously--suspecting him as the source--even as she felt its weirdness.

Now she watched as the blond and gorgeous Sandra Flynn, all in black, came down the church steps, a man on either side, and entered the second limo. A thickness rose in her throat, though no tears came.

At home, after knocking off five funereal paragraphs, she checked her mailbox, finding the oddest thing: a birthday card from the mourning widow with a note inviting her over the next morning at ten. Bizarre as that seemed (though indeed it was her birthday), Laureen pondered for less than a minute, then phoned back to leave a voice message that she would be happy to accept. Trying to relax, she opened a bottle of red wine, sliced up a chunk of yellow cheese, scattered some crackers on a plate, and sat down in front of the television. Once she finished the bottle, she fell asleep on the couch. When she rose at eleven the house was dark, as evidently Rodger had come home and turned off the set before going to bed at ten-thirty, his usual routine. So she undressed by the bathroom light as he lay there in oblivion. She washed and donned her flannel pajamas, then lay down next to him and slept again until after seven the next morning.

By then Rodger had already started for his eight o'clock class, probably taking breakfast in the diner on Veterans Parkway. He'd never said a word about her birthday, much less given her a card or a gift. Something was happening between him and her, all on account of the time she spent researching the scandal. She wasn't going to add his name to the list of those who troubled her. She didn't bother to ask herself if he'd forgotten her birthday last year or the year before. In the midst of this mess it was all the same to her.

She had her coffee alone, gathering the courage to visit Sandra Flynn, to whom she hadn't spoken in over ten years.

CHAPTER TWO
A Curious Oar

Her relationship with Mrs. Flynn was not the usual kind, and Sandra herself was what one might call, to be nice, eccentric. For Laureen there were mixed emotions here and mixed considerations.

Standing in front of the woman's impressive house, Laureen hit the button next to the dark oak door. At nine-fifty-five she was a tad early; then she recalled that her friend--if she might still call her that--would not be ready, since Sandra Flynn had always made people wait while she primped. Laureen, breathing impatiently, imagined the woman standing in the bedroom before a high triple-mirror still deciding what blouse or skirt to wear; even after those four chiming notes rang through the house, standing there in bra and panties brooding over the color of her lipstick.

She stepped back, looking up at the Flynns' Tudor-style home on Castlewood Path in the village of Belvedere--the North Shore enclave with its cream-colored French chateau gatehouse, and, a quarter mile down Bluff Lane, a semi-private 18-hole golf course and tennis club. She'd passed along this road any number of times during the last ten years and had always turned for a quick glance; and now, as if to reassure herself of what she already knew, and in spite of feeling conspicuous, she let her eyes travel up and down the two high gables that dropped slant-wise, crossing each other on either side of the smaller gable over the front door. Moving further back, she studied the dark brown crisscrossing beams higher up on the perfectly white stucco wall; complemented by the diamond pattern of the leaded windows and, lower down, the white diamond-marked green window-boxes filled with yellow chrysanthemums.

The architectural part of Sandra's existence was flawless. She couldn't wait to tell her friend how perfect the house had always seemed to her.

Still, a mild sadness came over her. She turned from side to side, surrounded by the disarray of brown leaves, unraked on the wide, still-green lawn and on the orange and russet leaf-clusters clinging above to the half-naked limbs of the high-reaching oaks: post-election autumn, she thought, a sweet-and-bitter ruin all its own.

It set the mood for the poignancy of Tom Flynn's death.

Sauntering here and there, she set her eyes on the painfully brilliant redness of the leaves bunched on two wide-limbed Japanese maple trees, trees so beautiful they reminded her of a mid-summer sunset. She stared at them, transfixed by unconscious memories. Vaguely, she heard a garage door lift and a voice call out to her:

"Are you there?"

She'd wandered about a hundred feet towards a wooded area. As she turned back and looked towards the front door, she saw no one. Disoriented--lost in a strange drama--she heard Sandra Flynn calling her from down the driveway and behind the house.

"Over here!" Sandra stood in front of the open garage, another, smaller Tudor structure, white with V-angled oak beams under a single gabled roof.

"Sandra," she called, walking swiftly to her, feeling her heart beating. "Lovely, really lovely," she added, "the house and everything."

In black blouse and jeans, her long blond hair falling over the collar of a black leather waist jacket, Sandra stared, expressionless. Laureen felt herself go ashen, hoping that she hadn't been over-loud or had sounded insincere. Tom . . . Tom, she began to say, but no words came. Sandra stared with those strange green eyes. Might Laureen finally see the inside of the house? In her heavy black overcoat she leaned forward, hand extended, while the shorter Sandra, with her chin up, swirled and marched into the garage.

"Wait here," Sandra called over her shoulder.

Laureen dropped her arm and bit her lower lip. On returning, the woman carried a gray weather-beaten oar, holding it with its blade upward. She posed with the thing and then said: "Here's something for your sensational detective work. Did you know that Tom shot himself with Uncle Arthur's silver Luger?"

"Uncle Arthur?"

"My Uncle Arthur, the politician, the Party Leader who drowned ten years ago?"

"The gun, yes." She meant the Luger, though not the original owner

This was queer. The suggestion of Uncle Arthur's drowning brought Laureen's thoughts away from Flynn's death and towards the freakish storm, ten, eleven years ago, in August before both of them got married, when the old man indeed had died.

"This is his oar. You remember the Flamingo Affair? That crazy business?"

"I'm so sorry," said Laureen, feeling an urge to cry. This all began so badly. Sandra seemed stressed-out; a little off-center; and Laureen's apology seemed to be for the deceased uncle, not Sandra's husband, though the listener may have taken them for both. Each woman looked away. Then each looked back.

"You don't understand," said Sandra: "There's a connection. See," she pointed to the oar-stem close to the paddle, "yellow and blue stripes; faded, of course. Those were his colors for everything, everything nautical, his yacht, his clothes, his flag. Well, this oar was on the boat when he fell overboard on the South Shore just beyond Shinnecock Inlet. His body washed up on Westhampton Beach the next morning."

"Of course, I remember," said Laureen. She'd written it up for the paper.

"They say his engine conked out? They say he used this to try and paddle his way back to land? They say he leaned too far over, and when the boat tipped sideways he got tossed in?"

Laureen nodded. Sandra's tone was childish and off-putting.

"This oar also washed up on the sand. Tom found it two months later on the beach and brought it home. He put it here in the garage, but he didn't tell me about it. That's when I knew he felt guilty--when I found it here, cleaning."

"Guilty? About what?"

"Guilty about my uncle. It wasn't only you; it wasn't only the scandal. It was this, too, Laureen." She shook the paddle. "Okay, so that was a long time ago. But you're a reporter. You find out things." She raised an eyebrow as if daring Laureen to go ahead and find out more about Tom Flynn and that old Flamingo Affair. "The tie he wore was yellow and blue. When he died." Then she glanced at the ground and looked up quickly: "That's all. I don't think we have much else to talk about."

As Laureen remembered, Arthur Weisskoff was a Party Leader in Suffolk County in the Eighties and Nineties. The man was close to his niece, Sandra, whose family seemed bent on suffering: accidents, nervous conditions, scandals. This allusion to Flynn's connection with the man's death seemed dull, farfetched: yellow and blue tie, indeed. It was a bygone episode. Laureen had reported on the incident at the time, even did some delving into the situation, but it was a crazy kind of drowning, apparently involving the controversy over the statue of a huge flamingo on the beach, angry neighbors, and an aging politician, Arthur Weisskoff, who thought he could handle the issue with a few deft pronouncements and a boat ride along the shore. There was a summer storm, and who could've been guilty of that?

"That's all? Okay," Laureen shrugged. "Very interesting. Thank you, Sandra. It's a shame. I didn't mean for this to happen."

Sandra's eyes drifted from side to side, as she muttered, "There was also something else here, and I . . . ."

She wandered back into the garage but didn't come out again. Laureen waited a few minutes, watching her misty breath exhale, then turned and walked back to her car. Of all the damned things. But what could she have expected when she'd just driven the woman's husband to . . . ? But was that it--that when he died Tom's tie was yellow and blue just like Uncle Arthur's oar? And the Flamingo Affair, that old thing. Desperate. Pathetic. Had the woman turned mystic? Not intriguing, just annoying. Driving home, Laureen began to suspect a better explanation. Did this abrupt, far-out business about the oar constitute Sandra's weird, subconscious intention to relieve her, Laureen, of some burden of the guilt over Tom's suicide? Even that seemed farfetched, and Laureen felt that sinking need again to escape from it all.

Once home she checked the Internet for articles on that nearly-forgotten Flamingo Affair: nothing. Then Rodger came in and started pacing around the house, checking for bad-weather cold spots. What was going on with him, she wondered. He'd been a law partner of the dead man, Tom Flynn, when they'd both graduated from Fordham Law School back in the mid-Nineties--a salt-and-pepper partnership the two would smartly joke about. But the arrangement broke up after Weisskoff's death, during the time he began dating her. Both he and Flynn were regulars in Weisskoff's party; but Rodger got a job as a Criminal Justice professor at Peconic College and quit politics; at about that time Tom switched parties, getting close with Frank Van Dam and his crew, as they gained on Weisskoff's party across the County.

Soon both she and Sandra were married, she to Rodger and Sandra to Tom. She'd started to feel confident as a journalist (she smiled to remember that she once thought of becoming a Suffolk County police officer); and gradually she settled into her marriage, that is, after a few bad bumps. It was strange how the past could rise out of nowhere, causing ripples in the present. She let her eyes rest on her husband as he knelt at the front door inspecting the weather-stripping at the base. He'd kept quiet during her writing about the missing money; but he must've known a lot about Tom Flynn, especially at that juncture in both their lives--and Arthur Weisskoff's.

And that silver pistol? Nothing.

Her thoughts wandered to Sandra, who had aged, gotten a little hippier, developed two deep worry lines between her eyes. But those eyes, those fascinating green eyes. They glittered on the surface when she'd smile, and then quickly, almost at the same time, they'd retreat into a wet, unfocused inwardness, as if called by something deeper and ill-defined. Sandra would always seem haunted in her beauty. It was this same fascinating ambiguity that Laureen faced now, just as in that time when the two were very close and about to say sayonara. Sandra, it seemed, wanted to say more of a personal nature, as Laureen could read in those green eyes, but she was evidently in the shock of grief--and of course anger over Laureen's rough handling of her husband. This little visit had been troubling; aggravating Laureen's sense of guilt, yet leaving her with the sense that if she couldn't get away, there might be something she could do, though what, she couldn't say.

As she sat up on the couch about to speak to her husband, the house phone rang, and she rose to pick it up in the kitchen.

"Hello, Laureen?" It was Sandra Flynn. "I'll make this quick. I'm sorry. I'm really sorry about this morning. Forgiven? Am I? Forgiven? You know, I just lost my husband, and I'm a little nuts these days."

"Okay," said Laureen, marveling at Sandra's rate of speech, the effect apparently of medication taken that afternoon, after she'd left.

"Okay? Good, good. Because I want you to come and see me tomorrow. At my house. I might have . . . I might have . . . . You see, I thought about having breakfast or lunch with you somewhere. But suppose we were seen? I mean, you and I, eating together. It would look pretty crazy. You know? So tomorrow morning at ten, all right? I'll have some bagels and pastry here."

Laureen stood musing. What else might Sandra have? When Rodger came into the kitchen to ask who called, she told him Joe Fallon, her boss at the paper. It went against her to lie, but the one subject that always got to him was Sandra Flynn. She'd told him about her before their marriage; he appeared barely interested: but that was over ten years ago when they were both in their twenties. As time went by, any allusion to her old friend brought a smirk to his face and some unpleasant remark, about either lesbians or white women or both. Laureen, therefore, kept a studied silence for the rest of the evening, through supper and through their desultory television viewing: downing three healthy glasses of wine, to Rodger's one, as she tried to think. When her husband went to bed at ten-thirty, she followed him. Neither of them fell quickly to sleep.

CHAPTER THREE
Old Friendship

Next day Laureen realized what Sandra meant when she suggested that it would look pretty crazy for them to be breakfasting together. She thought at first that Sandra had in mind their relationship of eleven years ago; but now she saw that she meant that the white wife of the dead man should not be found in a cozy chitchat over scrambled eggs and bacon with the black woman who'd supposedly driven him to his death. Again, that twinge of sinking guilt attacked her, causing her almost to swerve off the road. But she continued to Belvedere. There was that something else that Sandra mentioned; and also that something else that might be done.

Sandra greeted her at the door with a kiss on the cheek, then laughed. She patted down her pink V-neck sweater and smoothed her hip-hugging gray woolen skirt with pleats that fell from halfway down her thighs--an effect that brought attention to her shapely calves. "Come on," she beckoned, turning and leading Laureen into the house.

Laureen followed, smiling to herself, as she shut the door behind her. "No longer in black," she wanted to speak into her recorder, "Mrs. Thomas Flynn now appears in sexy pink and gray." Still, in the aftertaste of that twinge of guilt, she told herself to stifle the urge to sarcasm. She wanted, instead, to breathe whole again; finding a way out of the dilemma, out of the tragedy. This was the reason she'd agreed to chance a second encounter with Mrs. Flynn, who might be able to fill out her insinuation of a connection between Flynn and Weisskoff that yesterday seemed so odd, distant, and annoying--and yet mitigating of her guilt, if that were possible. Leading to murder, perhaps, instead of suicide.

She watched Sandra turn right and enter the living room. Then she followed. An expansive Persian rug in dark blue and red arabesques covered the floor. To the left, Sandra stood by a fireplace with a large painting of two horses, a black and a pinto, galloping across a meadow. In a black lacquered frame, it hung over a black-lacquered mantelpiece above two white porcelain clown figurines. To her right, on the opposite side of the large room, below the leaded windows with their inlaid wires patterned in Xs, was a capacious, overstuffed couch in bronze velour, accented with two large brown throw pillows imprinted with flying mallards. Four green cactuses with numberless spiny fingers climbed ceiling-ward behind the couch at the outline of the windows; the ceiling was high, sustained by old, rough-hewn wooden beams. Outside the window were the yellow mums; beyond them lay the front yard; and to the left, her car, and then further to the left the woods sloping down to the harbor.

The two women stood looking at each other--Laureen remembering that it had been a long time when they'd last talked seriously. She decided that the woman looked better than she first supposed. At thirty-four Sandra was well put-together: a blond with flowing, shoulder-length hair, full breasts and shapely hips, actually not much wider than ten years ago and still curvy. Her lips had that pouty look, as always. They were slightly sticky with a pinkish gloss; and her sulky expression was sexy, emphasized by those heavy eyelids. Laureen could overlook those two deep worry lines between her eyebrows. Sandra was still a beauty.

She wondered if Sandra checked her out, judging her as a thin, willowy sort who could never find a pair of jeans to fit or a cold-weather coat to hang on her gracefully. She assured herself, with her short black hair, straightened and pushed back over her ears, she could be as comfortable with men (this erotic business with Sandra had been a definite aberration) as her gorgeous friend by the fireplace; she, Laureen, had wide clear, dark brown eyes (black Irish eyes, her husband humorously called them) with long black lashes, high cheekbones, and naturally arched eyebrows. She had the charm of alert interest on her angular face, a virtue--so her mirror told her--that was always young and never old. Moreover, she had a warmth that was deep and personal. And everyone in high school had told her that she could have been a fashion model.

Two love seats faced each other before the fireplace, both in a leopardskin pattern. Sandra indicated for her friend to sit in one of them, as she would sit in the other. Laureen acquiesced. For all her self-consciousness, she prided herself on never letting anyone rattle her. From a certain age onward she'd developed integrity. It was she, as she reminded herself, who rattled others. Sitting, then, she leaned back with her chin raised and her head slightly tilted, holding her breath a bit. She would let her friend begin.

"Thank you so much for coming," Sandra said, with that sad look in her heavy-lidded green eyes.

"It's been a long time," said Laureen, who slipped off her overcoat, letting it rest behind her on the love seat. She dug her hips down, forcing herself to be comfortable on the cushion; she leaned familiarly forward now, clasping her hands, with her elbows on her knees. "I'd never seen your house, not the inside," she turned this way and that, letting her eyes roam around the room.

"No," replied Sandra, "that happened after."

Laureen said, "I'm impressed."

After a pause Sandra spoke: "Tom was a nervous guy, all right--and I should've known! But I can't believe he wanted to die! Suicide! And I didn't know. I didn't know. No, no, Laureen, I didn't see it coming!" And then there were tears.

Laureen leaned further towards her friend, shaking her head.

"Listen to me. Tom lost the election," the woman began again, "and so I thought that maybe he planned to leave town; go to Mexico or the Bahamas or Switzerland, wherever you think those stupid millions are stashed. Laureen, Laureen," her voice dropped into a whimper, "I know I seem crazy and shallow, but I thought I knew my husband." Then she whispered, "And it wasn't only the money."

"I heard he'd been drinking a lot," Laureen stated.

"True, true. He'd started drinking days earlier, and then I think he went and stayed in some motel on Route 347. I hadn't laid eyes on him since election night, and then he was dead!" Sandra stood still as she spoke, holding her hands before her as if pleading. "I hadn't seen him alive since he knew he lost. . . ."

In the long pause, Laureen could hear her own heart beating. "Now that you can think about it, it must seem possible, suicide," she said slowly. "Doesn't it?"

But Sandra shook her head more than a few times. She stared, then closed her eyes and opened them and said, "Would it be all right if I got a few more things off my chest?"

Sitting up straight, Laureen gestured for her to go ahead. She waited, forcing herself to breathe. She wanted to accept the pain.

Sandra launched into a nervous, whispered tirade about Laureen's failure as a friend: and, additionally, her failure to check her facts, her failure to see how she, Sandra, would take her attack on Tom, and her failure to see that nobody could win in a scandal except another set of bad guys. Laureen didn't answer; so her friend stared at her, blank-faced. Then dropping her face into her hands, the blond beauty fell to sobbing again. Just as suddenly she stopped, rose proudly, and walking around the back of her love seat, began to flick her hair away from her shoulders in quick, fluttery gestures.

Laureen watched. Then something moved within her; on impulse, she got up and walked around to her friend, embracing her from behind.

The blond allowed herself to be held; then bent over and wept again, hard, turning suddenly to her friend and falling into her embrace. Suddenly she stopped, stared into Laureen's face, and, pushing herself away, picked up a hairbrush lying on an end table. Walking back and forth in the space between the love seats and the bronze velour couch, she began to brush her long tresses with light downward strokes.

"You can't imagine," Laureen spoke, her arms extended, "how sorry I am. Sandra, I am so sorry. This is awful. I never intended . . . ." Embarrassed at having hugged her, she turned away and stared at the painting of the two horses running across a meadow. Time seemed to disappear. In the absence of conversation, Sandra stopped pacing, stopped brushing her hair. Still turned away, Laureen could hear her calming herself, drawing her breath in long, haling sounds.

Then she changed the subject, complaining that what stung her most was that she thought her friend had loved her once. How could she have been so insensitive, so egotistical to start this whole thing going? Was the Pulitzer Prize so important to her? To be gotten at Sandra's expense? And Tom's life?

Well, Laureen wondered, if it was suicide, what was the connection with Arthur Weisskoff's death and the suggestion that it wasn't only the money?

"How did Tom get a hold of your uncle's gun?" she asked.

The blond turned and went to the overstuffed velour couch to gaze out the leaded window. She kneeled forward onto the cushion, then turned and stared at Laureen, who came and stood near her. "He's gone." She waved her hand towards nowhere. Then she began to weep again, holding her head in her hands. "Gone, gone," she murmured. Then she remembered Laureen's question: "I don't know," she said. "The gun was in the house here. My uncle had given it to my father a long time back. So I gave it to him about a month ago. I was worried." She shrugged. She turned back to the window.

"Worried?"

Sandra shook her head: "Once your articles appeared, I sensed that something was up. In the party."

Really.

"What about the oar?" Laureen asked. "With the yellow and blue stripes?"

"Oh, that," answered the other, wiping her eyes. She stood and turned to her friend. "I hoped you could tell me."

Tell *her*? Tell her what?

Sandra stared ahead at nothing. Laureen sighed. There seemed to be another suggestion, something that Sandra was holding back. Something, perhaps, about the party?

Laureen waited. Sandra kept silent, turning and staring at her with her strange green eyes.

Laureen could not move. She could feel herself breathing. She stared off at the windows. Then she heard Sandra singing:

> "Momma's little baby loves short'nin', short'nin',
> Momma's little baby loves short'nin' bread."

She started to laugh. It seemed insane, until she remembered that this little touch of colored culture was Sandra's way of ending an argument, a sign to Laureen of her giving in and not wanting to fight any more. She was surrendering to Laureen's darker complexion, as a way of, well, what did it matter, it was so zany.

When the song stopped, a dullness descended on both of them. Laureen felt nostalgic; she imagined Sandra did too.

Sandra looked up at the taller woman, rising, coming close, and touching her arm. She had a melancholy in her green eyes that in the past indicated she wanted a drink . . . or something else . . . . Her touch had its effect. Laureen relaxed as her friend placed her hand on her cheek.

"Exotic thing," said Sandra, putting fingers of both hands on Laureen's cheekbones. "With your high cheekbones and that face, long and lean. You've always had a special attraction for me." Her fingers brushed Laureen's lips.

No, no, Laureen said to herself, drawing back. She stared at Sandra. She didn't want to panic, didn't want the conversation to end. But with a quick shudder, she turned and walked away towards the leopardskin love seats, where she grabbed her black overcoat. She moved too fast, she knew. She couldn't help herself. Something had begun that had nothing to do with Tom's death, and she felt incapable of accepting it: more than incapable, seriously anxious not to. With her overcoat on, she walked into the foyer and paused before glancing back at Sandra, who stood motionless in the middle of the Persian carpet.

"Maybe we could speak again," said Sandra, desolation in her eyes.

"Maybe. Not now. I'm sorry. Goodbye, Sandra."

"There was something else, but, no, I can't . . . . It's driving me crazy. But if I ever . . . well . . . . Goodbye." Her eyes spoke of a desperate need.

Laureen turned and left. No bagels, either, she commented to herself, remembering that Sandra had promised her breakfast.

Then as she started the car, she remembered: that something else; but it was too late now, whatever it might have been.

She gathered her breath while, above, the cloud-cover got lower and darker as the storm from the southeast gathered for certain tumult.

CHAPTER FOUR
The Flamingo Affair

On a whim as she drove home, Laureen stopped at the mall and walked into Victoria's Secret, where she bought a purple outfit for bedtime, panties with matching teddy. It wasn't her style to dress this way; but her thoughts had turned to her husband and the wasted hours, that is, the passionless hours she'd spent in bed with him since the beginning of the summer. At the same time she decided to ask Rodger some leading questions about the Tom Flynn and the Flamingo Affair.

The experience with Sandra Flynn set her going: she ought to look deeper into the case. Especially since a primary source could be sleeping next to her in bed.

Ordinarily, she wouldn't want to bring her husband into her work; but this wasn't work; and now that his name came up along with Tom Flynn's and Arthur Weisskoff's, she felt an obligation not only to herself but to, how else could she phrase it, the implications of the case, personal and otherwise. What do you do with two dead men hovering over your marriage? Yet she couldn't go running after him with questions. There was still the issue of their marriage. Those damned articles she'd developed during the late summer and early autumn months had their effect, so much so that conversation with Rodger had dried up; they'd pass each other in the house silently, and then go off to work; and then come home again to sleep. And that was all. Had they made love more than a few times since June? She couldn't remember the count, but it was low. Had they talked some politics, some theater, some music? She couldn't remember.

As it was, she'd noticed that Rodger's reaction to Flynn's suicide grew through the week. Day by day in a glum brood, he became more and more kinetic, pacing around, jumping from one topic to another, and looking for every little thing in the house to fix. Her quest for answers began after they had dinner in the kitchen. She asked him to sit with her and watch the evening news. There again was the film-bite of the casket's being placed in the hearse: the announcers now speaking of the Flynn and Weisskoff marriage and of the family's history in politics. So there was no avoiding talk about Tom and Sandra Flynn.

Laureen, leading casually into the issue, could see that all her comments about Arthur Weisskoff's death made Rodger nervous. He spoke vaguely. He admitted he was grief-stricken about Tom, as if hit hard in the chest. But there was more--this was evident--something to do with the partnership he and Flynn had before their marriage; something that involved Sandra's uncle, Arthur Weisskoff. It was there.

But suddenly he rose and began to pace about the house, the living room, the hallway, the kitchen. He inspected the sink, turning the spigot on and off, seeming to notice a drip that needed a washer. Just as suddenly, he changed his mind and exited out back, where she could see him walking around the yard, staring up at the roof, apparently at the gutters.

When Rodger came back, she mentioned something about taking a shower and inviting him in with her.

The man shook his head: it was only eight o'clock. Instead he turned and went outside again, to pace around the yard even as the weather got wild, with blustery gusts of rain. She showered alone. However, she was determined to get somewhere with the man, even at the cost of embarrassment. As she emerged from the bathroom, she wore the sexy outfit from Victoria's Secret, presenting herself as an object of coquettish desire. Rodger, as if by comical design, had re-entered the house and stood in the darkness of the bedroom doorway, his close-cropped hair dripping wet. And there they stood looking at each other, she tall and awkwardly tense in flimsy purple satin, lit faintly from the light on her night table, and he, turning aside as if he'd been too shocked to look, self-conscious about being caught in the rain and startled at her boldness. She herself stood there, posing, as it were, playful and girlish. She decided that she wouldn't be the first to speak.

Outside, the wind tore through the leaves, battering the house and pushing through at cracks with whistles and whines. They each looked towards the sounds, then back at each other: time for new windows, he seemed to say, raising an eyebrow, as if all he did these days was mend an old house. This was their one common reference: this Brentwood split ranch dating back to the 1960s. He shook his head disgustedly--always more to do, more to do.

"Gutters," he confirmed, as if he were a called-in repairman.

Her look told him that she wanted a half hour of sheer physicality, some understanding from her husband as to her status in the marriage. She wanted love. But beyond this, she was bargaining for something more, some leveling about his past in politics. For all she knew, he was still involved in something that might prove dangerous. Look at what it had done to Tom Flynn. Look at what it had done to Sandra. What was his problem: his friend's death; or, as Sandra had suggested, something deeper--something to do with Uncle Arthur?

The bedroom was semi-dark, with a low light coming from the lamp on the night table on her side of the bed; with moonlight flashing in at intervals between lulls in the rain. She walked to her side and knelt on the bed, gazing up at him. She opened her eyes wide and smiled; but he remained blank. He stood there fully dressed, breathing audibly, his face and hair still wet. Laureen felt a sinking of despair, but this would not stop her. It was she who, for the past few years, tended to initiate their coupling, though this was the first time she offered him the image of blatant sexuality. There'd been several times in the middle of the night when he'd awakened her with a raging desire; times long passed. She knew about, speculated about other women as distractions; but her warmth, actually, her intelligence, as she understood it, was the consistent element in his life, and with it she could always overcome his vagueness.

"You haven't kissed me in two weeks," she said smiling, allowing herself to speak now that Rodger had mentioned gutters.

He seemed to appreciate her get-up.

"You haven't kissed me, either," he replied, letting a smile come across his face. He went into the bathroom to wipe his face and hair. He was an undistinguished-looking fellow, and a bit too fretful; fretful in a way that cramped his features, bringing his eyebrows close and his mouth tight. Still, he had those sensitive watery blue eyes that contrasted so wonderfully with his brown skin; they brought out the caretaker in her, her forgiveness, as if in his softness she could feel her strength. When she married him, she told herself that her inch or two in height over him was not a question to bother with--they were two educated African Americans; they understood things together--yet she'd often found herself stooping when near him, and in bed she'd somehow tried to make herself smaller so as to make him seem more masculine--or else, perhaps, to make herself seem more feminine.

"Take off your clothes," she said when he came back into the bedroom.

He nodded, obeying. She waited, sitting now on the edge of the bed. Once undressed, he came to her side and stood over her.

She had to reach up to him to bring his face close to hers so that they might kiss; and now she eased onto her back, having him assume the superior position. Abruptly, however, when she became breathy he rolled onto his back, shaking his head.

"What's wrong?" she asked.

He lay staring at the ceiling.

"Okay," she said. "It's about Tom, isn't it? Tell me the truth. Talk to me, Rodge. Talk to me about Tom. I know there's more to tell. Tell me, tell your wife." She'd placed her hand on his chest.

"What do you want to know?" he asked.

"Whatever you know. All you know," she spoke softly, deliberately.

"As my wife or the *Newsday* reporter?"

"Rodge," she said, "be serious. We need to talk. You need to talk. To me."

He kept nodding until he jerked upwards and sat on his side of the bed, feet on the floor, his back to her, thinking. "I know," he muttered. "You're right, I know."

"He was your friend," she said.

"I know."

"Rodge," she continued, "you were partners."

"Right," he said.

A pause.

"And then you weren't."

"Right."

"You never went to his wake."

No reply.

The wind banged against their house, haunting in its whistle through the faults in the window frames. She'd always suspected that there was a racial issue somewhere in the break-up, but she could never get him to explain.

"Damn, damn that window," Rodger said, rising and pacing again, naked. "Nothing's ever done here!" Then, as Laureen waited for an explanation, the revelation of some long-kept secret, he launched into a tirade about the red-haired Frank Van Dam, how she failed to bring him to justice--was it because she'd dated him in high school; is that why? Grateful to the white man for all his attention to her? He was as guilty as the others, wasn't he?

"No proof," she said quietly. Was Rodger jealous of Van Dam, not because she'd dated him but because he'd stolen away his best friend? Because the two others were white and he wasn't?

"Don't be ridiculous," he answered.

There was more to learn about the switch Flynn made from the one party and Arthur Weisskoff to the other party and Frank Van Dam--and about her husband's leaving his partner Tom and his law practice and getting a job as a professor in Peconic College. There was always something she could never put her finger on. But he was going there, she could see, with this reference to Van Dam.

She got a white terry-cloth robe to cover her purple teddy. She sat in the armchair in the corner, giving him space to think.

"I'm sorry," she said. "Can we go back to the original topic?"

He didn't answer.

"I would never betray you, Rodge," she said softly. "This will stay private. As if you should even have to mention that."

As though struck with an idea, Rodger got himself into his dark blue terry cloth robe and immediately went to a window frame to see where the wind entered with its eerie noise. Having finished the inspection, he went to his dresser for a pair of white boxer shorts, his night-time wear, then came and sat at the foot of the bed. With both hands he began scratching through his damp, evenly-cropped black hair. She could hear his deep breathing. He stopped scratching. When he spoke, the words came easily as the recollection of an old dream.

There was a lot to the story that people didn't know. About Tom? No, about Arthur Weisskoff and his death at sea. Eleven years ago. As he paused, she remembered how Sandra, in her distraction over Tom, had alluded to her uncle, as if some irrational connection existed between one tragedy and the other. But after eleven years? Yet the way Rodger now said there was a lot to the story--it seemed to suggest that Weisskoff had been murdered and that he, her husband, knew something about who did it. Her excitement rose as Rodger continued, speaking slowly, thoughtfully. She was sure that he had some part in the Flamingo Affair that Flynn's death revived in him. It came, as it were, out of his pores.

Once in partnership after law school, they both decided, he and Tom, that there wasn't enough money in doing what the two of them were doing: putting criminals back on the street--not as long as illegal money could no longer be used to remunerate defense lawyers. Tom particularly was more ambitious, definitely set on being a judge before he was forty: "Either that or Governor," he'd exclaim, laughing. Tom had figured on his soon-to-be wife's relationship to Weisskoff--she being his niece--that they'd make faster headway politically, maybe gain a nomination, win a seat somewhere or get an appointment, eventually a judgeship. The problem was that Uncle Arthur moved slow. His candidates were used to winning local elections ever since their national party won most elections, twenty years back. And the Party Leader was in no mind to make waves with new ideas or grant favors to young dogs, as he called them, untested in their devotion to the party.

At this time a great fuss arose in the East End. An eccentric sculptor who billed himself as Stanko, his real name being Philip Stankowski, had created a thirty-foot-high pink flamingo, all made with loops of wire sealed in plastic, pink plastic. He named it The Flamingo. He proceeded to position this oversized bird on the sandy acreage in front of his home on Westhampton Beach, two hundred feet from the water. A hullabaloo ensued. There were circulated petitions and then town meetings and then newspaper reportage, written, in fact, by Laureen and her associates. And Tom, who'd been getting restless and looking for some way to irritate Weisskoff, thought it might be fun to hook up with The Flamingo supporters and bring the whole affair to a climax.

"It was a gay crowd, you know, from the East End," noted her husband. "You probably knew some of them. Well, you knew Stanko."

"True," she said. She'd interviewed him for the paper.

Through them, the crowd around Stanko, both Rodger and Tom hoped to bring Weisskoff into some kind of idiotic disgrace and formal retirement. The man was close to seventy and just hanging on from inertia. Against this, you had the ambition of young dog Tom Flynn and his intellectual black partner, young dog Rodger Metcalf.

"Art for Art's Sake": it was their tag, their secret joke, with its cute pun on Weisskoff's first name; and that became their title for the high controversy that followed, nearly splitting the party and initiating its decline in the county. Arthur Weisskoff hated art, associating it with homosexuality, *per se*. He wanted none of it visible in Suffolk County, especially not in the shape of a huge pink bird on a much-frequented beach known in part for its gay sun-worshipers. So both Rodger and Tom decided to support Stanko (or Stinko, as Weisskoff called him), who was grateful for this encouragement because the old man, as he and Tom called him, brought legal action against the sculptor to force him to take the great Flamingo down; and now Stanko decided to fight back. He had his own contingent of enthusiasts. So Tom suggested a public debate under the heading of "Art for Art's Sake," a suggestion that turned into a series of raucous town-hall meetings that drove the old man off his rocker.

The question came down to a duel between the old man and them; with the odds stacked against them, the young dogs. So Tom came up with another idea, as if to finish the case. He'd begun to turn to one desperate idea after another. Finally, he offered Weisskoff the "Challenge." Under newspaper coverage--Tom would first telephone *Newsday* and some local papers--they would go out in separate boats and officially view the thing from the water. Both men would meet about five hundred feet offshore and photograph The Flamingo to determine how much of an eyesore it was, and that would settle some part of the case, to what effect no one was sure. Of course, even then the business seemed absurd. But, again, Weisskoff was getting fudgy. He would foam at the mouth in any mention of The Flamingo; he'd do anything to destroy it.

To get to the meeting place on the water, the old man had to navigate Shinnecock Inlet about a quarter-mile between two licks of beach. Normally, no great task, but that morning it was rough and windy; and once into the inlet, his boat lost power, and he wound up overboard. He disappeared into the ocean. A few days later, some few miles east, parts of his body (or so the bones were assumed) washed up on the sand.

"And all this leads to?" asked Laureen.

It led to what appeared to be accidental death. Tom had been out, through the inlet, fifteen minutes before. He was anchored a few hundred yards off Westhampton Beach, offshore from the monster Flamingo. As the police discovered, the old man didn't have any gas in his tank. He had no more than enough to get started and go halfway through the inlet.

Rodger stood. He looked around the bedroom, his eyes unfocused. Then he turned to his wife.

"That's all the newspapers found out," he said. "The police didn't go any further."

He walked to the window. The turbulence outside bruited itself within. It felt like a huge force pounding and pounding; then whining and whining. Then it stopped. Rodger stood as if far away and continued.

When Tom returned and docked his boat, they noted what had happened, and the two stared at each other and limply shook hands. Then each of them smelled his own hand and cackled in a nervous, frightened laugh. They were scared.

"Having smelled gas . . . on your hand," said Laureen.

"As he smelled gas on his," reminded Rodger.

"So," she concluded, "You and Tom in some way murdered Arthur Weisskoff."

"After messing with the fuel line in his boat," he nodded. He shrugged. Then he rolled his eyes and inhaled deeply, letting out a heavy breath.

Laureen could feel her black Irish eyes expand as she asked the next question:

"Wasn't that a month before he married Sandra?"

"Something like that," answered Rodger, a slight smirk on his face.

"I remember."

"Of course you do. I mean, you wrote about the whole mess in the paper."

"Tell me more," she said.

"Nothing more," he replied, "except that I remember visiting him some months after they'd gotten married, and as he showed me around his garage with all its boating equipment I noticed the oar: the oar from Weisskoff's boat, with its blue and yellow stripe across the blade--it was the old man's colors; everything nautical with him was blue and yellow. Evidently, the old man tried to paddle his way out of the channel and, leaning too far over the side, got thrown into the surging water. Later, in October, after a storm, Tom and I took a walk on that beach. That's when he happened upon the oar, and Tom, after we left the beach, went back alone to get it for himself. As I found out on that visit, he wanted to keep it as a sort of souvenir, a *memento mori*, a reminder of death. Pure ghoulishness."

"And guilt."

He shrugged.

"Did you know that he wore a blue and yellow tie when he killed himself?" she asked.

He made no response. Perhaps he wasn't listening. He kept avoiding her eyes, glancing from one wall of the room to the other. He bit down on his lower lip and breathed deeply. "Coincidence," he said.

Laureen leaned forward, resting her elbows on her knees, looking down at the floor. She was afraid of continuing, but she said, "I'm here to listen."

Rodger's eyebrows got narrower. He nodded slowly. She waited, turning sideways to glance up at him.

"You want reasons? Okay. It was a prank," he muttered; "a prank," he repeated with a forced laugh: "Youthful . . . youthful . . . ." He dropped his head and breathed again.

"We were young. We figured the guy would bring a friend. Or at least check his fuel tank before starting. And we'd have a few laughs at that. And if anything went wrong, I mean, really wrong, we figured the old guy would be saved by the Coast Guard. He had a radio. He had life-saving equipment. It was summer. Whoever expected a high wind?" His watery blue eyes opened wide. He seemed surprised that it all came out so fast. "Weisskoff seemed invulnerable. The prank was a way to embarrass him--I don't know, to show how he flubbed the challenge. He was stupid enough to fall for it. It was bad; it went wrong, way wrong."

He'd been gesturing with two hands, symmetrically. He began to run his fingers through the hair on both sides of his head. He breathed deeply through his nostrils. Then he sat on the edge of the bed away from her. From her position on the armchair, she wanted to reach and touch him, but she didn't. He was settling things within himself. That's what his breathing showed, as his shoulders rose and fell. He'd relieved himself of an old burden, but the sin of it disturbed him still, and where was he to go with that?

Laureen remained silent. She began shaking her head, not sure of what to feel. For the moment she felt nothing except pity, but for what or whom she wasn't clear. She kept saying to herself, he's my husband, he's my husband-- but also, he did it, he really did it.

In the dim-lit room, with the winds in motion outside the ill-framed windows, his guilt seemed to seek out and hover in the dark spaces, in the door frame, in the corners, and alongside the dresser. She had always sensed an edginess in Rodger, a part of him that couldn't relax and wouldn't reveal itself; and, more, she somehow knew that this had an association with his old friend, Tom Flynn. For why had he avoided the man? And why had Tom Flynn left one party and joined another? Flynn, too, seemed to be averse to an old friendship. Not till now did it all come together for her, though not entirely. The thought of Rodger's guilt, old as it was, brought to mind the question of the moment: that Tom Flynn's death may not have been a suicide.

As if Tom, now in trouble with the law, would finger Rodger in another case to buy himself some time. And her husband, seeing that possibility . . . .

But, no, even if someone had deliberately killed the man, Tom's murderer, if any there was, could not have been her husband--an idea not to be thought on. She knew her husband. If he was bad, it was in other ways. He was not a criminal. Not even in Weisskoff's death, which, after all, was an accident. If he was guilty of that, it was not by his intention. But how messy it was. Suddenly she was overcome by a need to escape. Why hadn't she arranged for some kind of trip, if not to Costa Rica at least to Mexico? Obviously, because she'd grown heart-dull and stupid in the past few months, blaming her husband for keeping her here. Now she wanted to just go. She didn't want to get involved in any more complexities, least of all in the realm of murder--or the nuances of her husband's guilt. She didn't care now if Rodger came with her or not. On the other hand, she felt she couldn't leave him alone, not now.

She felt something, a pain at her own ambivalence--this was what came from asking questions--and a resentment at Rodger's waiting so many years to confess.

The digital clock on her nightstand read one o'clock. It was time to sleep.

"I'm sleepy," she lied, removing her robe. "Let's rest."

Rodger slipped off his robe. He flipped back the covers and lay down. They lay still for a while, until she began to touch him, to arouse him. She removed her panties; he his undershorts. With that, she drew him over her. Suddenly he kissed her hard several times and then entered her, breathing heavily. The act was quick and desperate; earnest if brief, yet not so intense as she wanted it to be. Afterwards she felt restless, empty. He kissed her again, then lay back down on his side of the bed.

"We let ourselves make mistakes," he said after a while. "There's no way to undo them."

She supposed he referred to the prank with Tom Flynn. She could think of others. There was that incident of the black panty hose in the backseat of his new Ford, five years ago. She wondered if there was anything recent. She clicked off the light on her nightstand.

"If it weren't for that damned Flamingo," he whispered. "Stupidly enough, it keeled over some time that October in a terrific nor'easter. The sand underneath gave way. Who'd've predicted? It was made of pink plastic over metal wire. A good part of it was rusted. You could barely see the rust, though, for the pinkish color. There was something sick about it. It would have fallen sooner or later. We'd all been real idiots."

As the rain stopped, an eerie quiet crept into the room. In the chiaroscuro darkness an indefinable shadow of a large branch moved back and forth against the wall opposite the window. Laureen tried to connect the Flamingo Affair with

Tom Flynn's death, putting pieces together from what she knew about politics, but she'd become tired. She felt afraid. Even more, she felt the rising need to close herself off and go into a deep sleep. But there was no way, not tonight.

And her husband, lying next to her, continued to whisper. "Weisskoff hated us for challenging him. All he had to do was wait us out. How many tricks could we play? But not him. He had to take his craft, as he called it, and motor out to survey the thing, as if he owned the coastline. I remember wondering if you'd be there to report on it--I'm sure *Newsday* intended to send somebody. But nobody came out until after it was over. We were alone when the storm broke. Where were you? Weren't you supposed to be there?"

She couldn't recall. All she remembered was the noise and fuss in the office when the news came in: Arthur Weisskoff, drowned. She remembered that previously Rodger had phoned several times to feed her bits of information during the course of the Flamingo Affair. She remembered their first coffee date, how sheepish he seemed and how, at the same time, fastidious: a young, ambitious black guy in suit and white shirt, a perfect knot in his tie, emitting a faint odor of the latest men's cologne. She'd considered him something of a political punk--hardly dangerous.

"So he died," Rodger concluded, a pathetic touch of incredulity in his voice. "And the bird toppled over. A flamingo on Long Island. When I saw it in the sand, rusty, with its sick pink color, I started to run. I must've run a mile on the beach before I stopped: I knew I had to get out:

I never felt so . . . racial. Later I met Tom back at the car. That's when he'd found the oar, and showed it to me. I wouldn't touch it. I told him to throw it away; and he did, for that moment. I told him I was getting out, and he laughed. There was something about you then, Laureen. I was ready to move to Canada; I had that cousin in Toronto; but you were there, and I decided to stay and accept a teaching job. Tom, on the other hand, lived in denial. He'd made plans, supposing that if he didn't get to be Governor he could at least become a judge. He was vain. He'd found Frank Van Dam, you know, and they got each other into money and power. And then last week they found him."

The connections kept coming. Even she, Laureen, was part of that agenda. Had he loved her, she wondered, when he asked her to marry him? But then, but then why had he done what he'd with this one and that one? There definitely were several. No, she wouldn't go into to all that again, not now. But, yes, there was that prime incident of the black panty hose stuffed into the seat in the back of the car.

She looked over at her husband. He'd grown quiet; perhaps he'd fallen asleep. His face had drawn even more tensely into itself as if he were trying hard to get at something lodged within.

CHAPTER FIVE
The Briefcase

Still in awe of his confession, she saw him in jeopardy, though of what she couldn't be sure. She had opened the can of worms, but where was she to go with it? She saw, then, the need for mutual support that called for her to say something as well.

The next evening she told Rodger about her own touch of guilt in the death of Tom Flynn. They sat in a restaurant, and Rodger smiled as she spoke, then assured her that she had nothing to feel guilty about. She didn't kill anyone; the man killed himself. The way he said it made her laugh, until she realized that his sentiments barely touched what she felt.

So she spoke about her brief second visit to Sandra Flynn. She told him everything, even her uncomfortable feelings when the woman gazed at her and touched her. She believed he might feel closer to her. At this moment they each needed that.

Head down, he continued to eat his veal chop quietly, chewing slowly, avoiding her with his eyes. He sipped his wine carefully. She mistook his silence for sympathy. Once home, however, he went into a tirade. He couldn't believe she could do this, couldn't believe she could do that--and then smilingly confess to everything!

"I thought you and she had ended it," he snarled.

"I was stupid, I admit; but, as I told you, I hadn't seen her in over ten years." She was shocked that he could be so hard, so self-righteous. "Nothing really happened."

"Right," he said, as if she'd been cheating on him all along.

How was your girlfriend, that studious Lolita? she wanted to ask. And those others? He had no comprehension of how his extra-curricular activity had hurt her. But that had been hashed over many times before. Time had passed. Five years. Yet those things weren't fiction. She determined to stop thinking; she tried thinking of nothing. She looked at him as if to say that she'd told him everything. She'd accepted him fully. She'd allowed herself to be vulnerable. Please, she thought to herself, please understand. She paused before she added, I love you, but only to herself. His face had grown stony.

"You promised me," he said, his chin jutting forward. He nodded rhythmically. "How am I supposed to accept this . . . this lesbianism?"

"Monday was my birthday," she said after a long pause.

He blinked but gave no reply.

Her jaw got tighter. She was alone. She looked away and mumbled that she was tired and had a headache and needed to go to bed.

In the morning she awoke in turmoil over her husband's part in Weisskoff's death, she deciding that his crudeness in speaking about Sandra left her without any guilt in drawing his confession out of him and also with a certain freedom of action: specifically, another visit to Sandra. She considered if there was something more she could find out from the widow, such a visit might relieve her of the uneasiness of having visited her before--as well as for the guilt in Flynn's death. It would be a revenge for the nasty judgment Rodger leveled against her.

Did she not have a duty to go back? In retrospect the connection between the oar and Tom's tie seemed less farfetched; and then there was that indefinable something that brought Sandra to contact her--something else, perhaps, substantial.

She phoned the widow.

"Yes, of course," replied Sandra. "I have those bagels I promised you. You can have coffee . . . or something else, if you want. We can have a nice, happy brunch."

The two-day storm had fled. The sky was sunny and bright. Sandra met her at the door, smiling. In the kitchen they munched on cream cheese and bagels. Laureen had nixed the woman's suggestion of Bloody Marys; so Sandra shrugged and made a carafe of ten cups of fresh coffee.

After the second cup Laureen asked about her friend's suspicions in Tom's death. And the gun she gave Tom? She thought she'd been pretty direct. But Sandra put down her bagel and stared at her friend for a while.

"Thank you," said Sandra, "for coming back. For not hating me."

Laureen looked up.

"God, I've thought of you," Sandra whispered, "when everything flies at you from everywhere and there's nothing to hold onto: I knew you'd come again! I knew you cared. I knew your editor put you up to all that, and I knew you'd felt guilty, just enough to want to help. You couldn't refuse an old friend who needed you and whose husband . . . ." Her eyes assumed that haunting inwardness. Directed at Laureen, they glazed over, unfocused.

Then she rose from her chair and came towards her and, leaning over her, said, "Look at me," as she planted a long kiss on Laureen's lips. Laureen tossed her head free, flushing. She wiped her mouth with a napkin and stood.

"You can't be doing that," she said, her eyes wide. "That's not why I came!" The visit became illegitimate, dangerous. She felt a pang of betrayal and disgust: and here was Sandra, with a sickly, knowing smile, shaking her head. Was there any justice in Rodger's lack of sympathy? For Laureen had come back for explanations, facts, questions about suicide, and possibly murder. Not old romance. Isn't that what Sandra had understood? Had she in some way lured Sandra on? No. This was all Sandra.

"Who needs a peck on the cheek at the door?" Sandra laughed. "Besides, I felt the impulse. I remembered those lips." Her eyes glittered.

"I thought you grieved for your husband," Laureen sucked in those lips and straightened the collar on her white blouse.

"Him?" Sandra laughed. "He's gone. What can he offer me? Nothing, not anymore." Her eyes grew ambiguous. Her flippancy was disturbing; as if grief had a weird privilege: this playful detachment, this sense of spurious fun that Laureen once found crazy and irresistible. But now, as if it were all over, the death, the funeral, the period of mourning. As if the death never happened. As if . . . they'd never said goodbye. As if what they might do next was retire to the bedroom.

Panicking, she coughed and shivered. She had to leave . . . again.

She'd been hoping . . . that there was no suicide but maybe evidence that Sandra held back, involving other people! That there was a third or fourth party beyond Tom and Uncle Arthur and Rodger at Shinnecock Inlet! She'd expected to hear more about the connection the other had hinted at between her husband and her uncle--the connection in deaths--beyond the yellow and blue tie that Flynn had worn on his death-day. Some evidence beyond that oar in the garage. What idiocy! And crazily, she admitted to herself, she realized a need to protect her husband. Given his tendency to nervousness, given the racial situation and the law, there was a serious threat to her vulnerable, if stupid, husband. In spite of everything, she needed to find something to deflect it.

She moved toward the hall without turning, aiming herself at the clothes closet, where Sandra had hung her overcoat; and once retrieving it, she relaxed, slipping into it. She turned and faced her friend.

"No, Sandra. That's all in the past. I thought I wanted you then, but honestly it wasn't for me." Her voice was toneless. "When I received your card the other day I decided to come but only to help you. Help myself, too. Oh, it was a long time ago." She shook her head. She felt that "long time ago" in the depths of her chest.

"Eternity," breathed Sandra.

"We were stupid and careless." At the time, Sandra had been an expression of her youthful feminism. That is, the sexual Sandra; for she'd always liked her as a friend, a white girl who offered her a loony freedom from responsibility--and then someone whom she allowed one night to cross the barrier that separated mere friends.

"And I was shallow, I know," admitted Sandra. "And Tom, that nice boy, was always nearby, and he had a smile with perfectly white teeth and light brown hair that used to fall over one eye. And he was going places. He wanted to get married and have a child. So we got married." She paused, then dropped her head into her hands and, as she had two days ago, sobbed unrestrainedly. As with Laureen, there'd been no children.

"You must remember that I was the one who said goodbye to you."

"You're right," nodded Sandra, wiping her eyes; "I never closed the door! I don't know how to close a door! Tom always yelled at me for that." Her smile made her teary eyes glisten.

"You had something serious to show me?" Laureen deadpanned. She asked about the silver Luger

The other stood away, wide-eyed, lovely in this new outfit, light and dark green, even with the smeared mascara around her temples. Yes, it was better to leave now, Laureen decided, feeling stupidly compromised--and blaming herself for this second, or now third, visit.

"Oh," said Sandra, "I don't know. Something about Van Dam, was it?" She sighed.

Was everyone around her just stupid?

As she turned, Sandra embraced her from behind around her waist, pressing her cheek against her friend's back.

"No, don't leave, not yet, not again. I do have something for you, something real," she pleaded. "Turn and look at me. Laureen, please."

So the other gave in and turned; and the widow reached for and held both of her hands, gazing meaningfully into her friend's dark eyes. "After the election, when I realized Tom had left the house," she began slowly, "I began to remember. Come," she dropped one hand while still holding the other; "and take off your coat and, please, leave that purse on the floor": and, Laureen obeying, led her from the entrance hall up the stairs and into her bedroom.

Skeptical but not resisting, Laureen followed until she stopped at the bedroom doorway, leaning against the doorpost. She sighed. The relationship had for her a curious pain she needed back then. Nothing had changed. Here was the same wild, beautiful Sandra, all dazzle and no substance. It was not for her, Laureen, not then, and not now. She'd wanted for her life to be . . . something else. Glancing around the bedroom, she saw how neatly every item stood in its place, toiletries, photos, two books placed carefully on the lower shelf of the bed-table--no pantyhose on the thick pink carpet, not even a piece of lint! If only the woman's mind was anything like her housekeeping, what a wonder she'd be!

Sandra spoke in a high-pitched, friendly voice. "Come here," she beckoned with a jerk of her head; "look at this."

From the distance of the doorway, Laureen saw a brown leather briefcase: a zippered one. Sandra held it open, shaking her head, indicating there was something in it. "Look, notebooks."

"Whose?"

"Tom's. He kept pages in this with lots of writing."

"Really?"

Sandra nodded.

Laureen advanced across the pink carpet . . . to take the briefcase and inspect it. It was heavy with four or five spiral notebooks. The beautiful one assumed a coy, helpless look, relaxing her shoulders and looking up at her tall friend.

"I found it where I found the oar. In the garage. I knew he had it there. I'd check on it from time to time. Part of it is a diary, about politics, about politicians, but I'd never read it, not more than quickly once or twice. So boring. But with Tom gone, I went there a few days ago to check on it again right where . . . well, squished behind some old boxes. Really."

"What's written in it?

"Lots of stuff."

"You should've Xeroxed it."

"He only just died, Laureen. I just came across it again. I'm not sure what I read."

"Right."

"And I'd give it all to you, but . . . but first I want to read it again. One more time. Now that I feel clearer. Then I'll send you the good parts. I think there are good parts."

"Right."

"Just give me a day or two."

"Of course."

Laureen handed the briefcase back. She wanted to suggest that they re-read it together. But no. That might involve . . . no, no, no. Instead she sat on the edge of the bed, speculating. "Interesting. Anything about money?"

"Probably. I think so."

"Well," Laureen rose. She had to go home and think. This diary-revelation was overwhelming--suggesting the possibility that Tom Flynn may have been murdered after all. For his diary.

"Don't go yet," Sandra held out an arm as if to bar her way. "There's another item, perfectly innocent, that I want to show you."

After tossing the briefcase on the bed, she lifted a framed photo from its place on her dresser and held it out. There they were, a younger Laureen and Sandra in swimwear on a beach.

"Look. Among the family photos, look what I keep on my dresser--well, in my dresser, face down, during the campaign. That's you and me. On Cape Cod. Our little excursion. The summer before Tom, before Uncle Arthur's troubles, remember how cool it was? Nobody went in the water. People sat around on blankets taking each other's picture. We walked and walked that day. And we saw this long-legged bird splashing on the shore. I asked you if that was a flamingo. It was my first time in New England. I thought all faraway beaches had flamingos. And you thought I was stupid."

"It was not a flamingo." Did Sandra, in her madness, now have a peculiar connection to flamingo episodes? Or was it her, Laureen's, fetish to take note of them?

"But you didn't know what it was either. At least I took a chance at guessing. As we tried to take its picture, the bird flapped its wings and flew to another part of the beach, and we followed after; but it flew again, and again we followed, and it flew again. By now there were boys on the beach, and we asked them to take our picture; then we asked if they knew about large birds, but they only shrugged. So I continued to call the bird a flamingo. Until you got angry. You refused to hold my hand. So I wondered what we were doing there, walking on the beach, a study in black and white. You said you didn't know, and I said the same thing. Then you said we shared a love, and I said, 'Flamingo love.' Then you laughed and said, 'Yes, flamingo love,' because it was strange, and we couldn't walk away from it."

She did of course walk away from it; still, a heaviness pressed on Laureen's chest. She did not want to remember this, did not want this awkward nostalgia. But the memory was vivid: actually, the only good one. Yet it was only a memory. It was insubstantial, like their strange, short-lived romance. It was part of the dead past, and yet, she had to admit, thoughts of the past made her moody from time to time. And now these old, confused feelings. And Tom's sudden, disheartening, and terrible demise. And Rodger's confession. And his crudeness. She let Sandra hold the photo; she didn't touch it.

"I did love you once," she confessed, shrugging and looking off, "for a while."

"Love me again," Sandra whispered, putting the frame down on her dresser "Because that's how I feel about you, in spite of everything."

Laureen stood motionless as the other came and kissed her on the cheek. So this, finally, was the destined moment.

"I would never be that crazy," she said.

Sandra gazed up at her with those lovely green eyes.

"But you could be, you could," she breathed.

They kissed on the lips. Sandra held her for a long time and then began to undo the buttons on her friend's blouse and open the front of her bra. She went unresisted until she placed her lips on Laureen's small bare breast, when her friend pushed her away and said, "No."

They stared at each other for a long time.

"Then why?" Sandra asked, still staring, indignant. Her eyes took on an obscenely scary expression. What was she insinuating? Why what? Why did Laureen work so hard to do away with her husband?

Suddenly the house phone rang. Sandra didn't answer it and instead hurried out of the bedroom and downstairs to the living room. The ringing stopped, and Laureen could overhear the woman's voice go quickly from friendly to business-like.

"Yes? Oh, hello. What? Yes, yes, I'm fine. Thank you for asking. I'll be all right. Yes, I guess so. Listen, I have company. We'll talk again, okay? Goodbye."

Buttoning up, Laureen tried to be nonchalant: no running away in hysterics. She needed those notebooks. As she descended the stairs, Sandra hung the phone up in a wall niche and turned to her.

"That was Van Dam," she said. "About Tom." She paused, allowing the information to settle. "He wanted to be sure I was all right."

Laureen cocked an eyebrow, leaning her head to one side. Him.

"He supposed I might want to have lunch with him this week," Sandra continued. "What a moron."

"You're not cozy with him, are you?"

"I don't think so," replied Sandra. "He's always been nice to me in a pain-in-the-ass kind of way; that's about it."

"And you and he never . . . ?"

The widow smiled. Cutely, weirdly.

Drained of feeling, Laureen leaned against the entrance to the living room, looking at Sandra. The tense moment had passed; they were detached now, these two intimate friends of many years ago. Yet how could this widow have suggested, rather insinuated . . . ? Loose in the brain was what she was.

"I said a pain in the ass," Sandra apologetically, staring up at Laureen. "You bat your eyes at a guy, and he thinks he can take you to bed."

Interesting. And then another thought ran through Laureen's head and she asked, "Van Dam was cozy with both Tom and Rodger, wasn't he, when your uncle drowned?"

"Of course," said Sandra. "That's what I've been trying to tell you!"

"Our husbands were pretty good friends," Laureen said. "Before we all got married. Though they never spoke much after."

"True," said Sandra. "And neither did we."

Thank God, the other said to herself; and then: "Well, what about Tom and Rodger and your uncle? And Frank Van Dam? How does the Boy Wonder fit in?"

"I don't know. Something in those notebooks maybe. I thought you'd be able to put things together. You'll see, maybe, when you read what's in them," Sandra raised an eyebrow and shrugged. "Nothing's clear to me. Just stuff here and there. And then just some crazy suspicion when I saw the tie he wore; when they returned it to me in the morgue."

"And Van Dam?"

"Oh, come on, Laureen, I know about you and Van Dam," Sandra laughed with forced sarcasm, "ha ha ha."

Full of implication this morning, Laureen noted. She could have shrugged off the ha ha ha, except for what had gone before and what she and Sandra both knew was the suggestion that she went soft on Van Dam because she'd dated him in high school. Dated him, that is, and had a night with him that she regretted so much she wouldn't see him afterwards . . . for reasons that Van Dam would have to explain. And that was twenty years ago! Now that revelation between girlfriends was suddenly thrown at her as an accusation. But, no, Laureen did not go after Tom Flynn in order to get back with Sandra; just as she would never catch herself being soft on Frank Van Dam--and Sandra should have known that. Moreover, there was no sign that Van Dam had any of the missing money. Rather there was that strange sense that he'd helped her, feeding her secret information about the guilty ones, perhaps because . . . because he'd wanted to keep from being drawn into the whirlpool. But even as he lost an election? Improbable. And yet . . . he was nothing if not improbable. So what if he lost the election this year; he'd be back. He was the Boy Wonder! Even so and most of all, could he be the chief villain? That thought had plagued her for the past four months. Sandra seemed firmly to think so. Even if Sandra and he had once . . . . Yet if only . . . if only Sandra could help her prove his guilt. If only this diary . . . if only Sandra were coherent . . . even slightly objective.

Still, stupidly, Sandra had always been jealous of Van Dam. And way off the mark. If anyone fixated on him it was she, Sandra, whose husband worked hand-in-glove with him and who Sandra, from her bitterness in seeing Tom fall as Van Dam went free, needed, perhaps, to bring him into guilt as well.

In fact, Sandra's insinuations seemed to cover up her own possible guilt. Had she been hoping for her husband to die; and had she been to bed with the Boy Wonder? Very possibly, knowing Sandra. Had she and Van Dam plotted Flynn's murder and made it look like suicide? Then planned to destroy the diary, once it was found, together? No, no, not Sandra: too fluttery, too loony. Nobody could plan a murder with her as an accomplice. And here, she'd just shown Laureen the diary! Why wouldn't she just give it to her?

There she was with that brush again, walking back and forth to the bronze velour couch, glancing out the window, then back at Laureen while attacking her hair with great deliberate, downward strokes.

"Stop brushing your hair as if you were clawing at it. Long strands are dropping all over your shoulders," Laureen said.

"You care?" Sandra whimpered. "About my hair?" Tossing the brush onto the couch, she did something grotesque, pressing her fingers against her cheeks, pushing the skin back and upward against her ears, appearing like a Halloween mask. She held the pose as if awaiting a reaction.

"Kitty Van Dam," she said when Laureen looked blank. "Kitty Van Dam said the same thing to me one night." The taller woman looked blank. "The wife of Frank Van Dam? Our noble leader? The man who'll get the seventeen million? The man you wished you married?" As Laureen failed to respond, the other continued: "Well, one night at a big dinner, Kitty Van Dam turned to me with her new, cosmetically uplifted face and said, 'Did you know your hair is falling out?' "

"Seriously?" Laureen laughed and, stepping closer to Sandra, began to pick the strands from the green v-neck sweater. "Tell me all about Kitty Van Dam." The woman had kept a low profile for years.

The story on Van Dam's long-suffering wife was that she'd taken a two-week end-of-summer vacation to Peru and just come back a totally altered human being: Botox lips, tightened eyelids, smoothened wrinkles on the neck, no more love handles--"all the fat sucked out." And now there was nothing natural about her. "Survival of the fittest," added Sandra.

"Survival of the unfittest," said Laureen. They both laughed.

"She's your age," commented Sandra, "but she's always looked ten years older than Frank--who's also your age."

Surely, it was Sandra who couldn't stop thinking about the Boy Wonder, that smooth-talking friend of her husband's. Laureen was quite sure that she herself cared nothing about him.

"Sometimes these things never resolve themselves," Sandra had gone off on another tack that the other picked up in mid-stream. "Besides, Tom and I were faithful in our fashion. He had his political friends, and I have, had, booze. Both can lead to trouble. I've cured mine."

"Yet when you kissed me," Laureen said, "just now."

"You detected alcohol on my breath? You're just like Tom. Maybe I should have had a chocolate mint with my coffee."

"Instead of a crème de menthe with your toothpaste?" deadpanned Laureen. Both laughed. But Laureen stopped first. "Why are you so fucking weak?"

"Am I not fit for survival?" Sandra asked, puckering her lips, looking comical in her smeared mascara. They both laughed again, briefly.

Then each avoided the other's eyes.

"I'll mail you the interesting pages," Sandra murmured.

Quietly, with a slight nod, the other turned and, picking up her coat and purse at the bottom of the stair, walked to the front door. Sandra came and stood by the entrance to the living room. Laureen, feeling that she'd wandered astray, pulled herself into her black overcoat and, glancing back at her friend, nodded once more. She had the heart-deadening sense that they would never see each again. Her green eyes unfocused, Sandra too seemed full of regret, as if she understood, without looking, the meaning in her friend's impassive face.

Outside, the air had gotten very chilly.

CHAPTER SIX
Pheromones

That afternoon she and Rodger didn't speak. While they ignored each other, Laureen was glad to notice that he wasn't as jumpy as he'd been. After dinner he sat silently at the end of the couch and let her change channels casually. She fell asleep. When she awoke, he'd already retired. She went to bed at midnight.

Tired as she was, Laureen lay saying to herself, "Can't sleep, can't sleep, can't sleep," and now on Saturday morning she saw that she'd overslept. When she awoke at nine, her head was heavy; still, she felt a clogged urgency. All she could think of was the leather briefcase and its four or five old notebooks. She wondered what they might reveal--and if Sandra would mail the critical pages to her or was, rather, in the process of negotiating with someone about their contents. Perhaps they were just law school notes. About money? When her speculations ended, all she could think of was Rodger. Then all she could think of was Frank Van Dam.

As she rose from bed, she noticed there was a message on her telephone.

Sandra spoke: "Laureen, Laureen, I'm sending you ten or fifteen pages. Ripped out. No time to Xerox. They'll be in the mail. You need these. Money, money, money."

The call was from seven-thirteen a. m.

That woke her up. She phoned Sandra but got no answer: not home, probably out mailing the envelope. She'd have to wait. Meanwhile there was Rodger. And too much to think about. Those notebook pages might involve him as well as the money.

Rodger's high-handed attitude suggested to her that something was wrong, either with what he'd done or was about to do. She squelched an impulse to search through his closet--and the rest of the house--for stuff he may have written. No, no, she told herself: too creepy; some other time. Besides, she was fearful about what to do if she did find anything. Her head began to ache.

Anxiously, she wanted to question him again, but he was not in bed or anywhere in the house. Perhaps he'd gone off to grade papers in his school office, something he did on Saturday mornings. She would call him after breakfast. They could have lunch together at the Mexican place in Commack. Perhaps there was nothing wrong, and he'd be in a better mood. Perhaps all was healable between them as well as between him and the world. If only that could be. Was she verging on paranoia? Then she began sneezing after her second cup of coffee, and then her nose began to run. She wondered if she should go back to bed. And then she worried about losing track of things. Fretting that Sandra might call again while she slept, she stayed in the kitchen and got herself another cup of coffee.

Sitting still and looking back, she tried to put some meaning to the catastrophes of the past weeks: to Rodger's guilt (where did it end?), to Sandra's craziness (how un-crazy was it?), to her own, what was it, part in the tragedy.

Her memory turned to her visiting the morgue to see Tom Flynn's body last Tuesday, the day after his death.

She hadn't wanted to go, especially not alone. This was the day after the suicide. She'd thought her work was over with the report on the death scene. She'd phoned her editor, Joe Fallon, out of habit, only to hear him tell her to drive up to Hauppauge and check out Tom Flynn's body in the Center for Forensic Sciences, a.k.a. the county morgue. Fallon had called Chris Steiner, the Assistant Chief Medical Examiner, who'd given him the okay. A minute later, after she refused, after she awkwardly hung up, her editor called her back, and told her to do what she had to do as quickly as possible. This was her story, and the newspaper needed it. She could take a look, maybe get a photo. Did she understand?

"Didn't you see the headline?" Fallon had asked.

"No."

When she got the paper from her driveway, she'd read, "Suffolk Shock: Flynn Shot Dead, Suicide?" Her story was on page three, with two photos of Flynn's office she'd taken herself. Nothing she mightn't have expected. It wasn't a surprise anymore, but it was then that her chills started.

With a heavy sweater under her black overcoat, Laureen continued to feel chilly, even with the heater in the car at full blast. It was the first nasty day of late autumn; but it was more than that. The chill persisted even as she entered the building in Hauppauge where Tom's body lay in a sterling silver drawer, feet extended back into the cabinet, head towards her. She began to shiver as she saw the wound, a large purplish crater-like gash, in Tom's head. One eye was closed, the other half-open, bulging under the eyelid, and leaning to the side as if trying to find a way out. Laureen began to get woozy, but the young, stocky blonde-haired Chris Steiner, suave in his blue lab coat, put his heavy arm around her, and she began to breathe again, her head clearing and her body feeling warmer.

"I usually don't over-react," she explained. But this was her first time alone with the dead. Usually she came with a small group of police and fellow reporters; and even among them she'd hang back from the body.

Chris Steiner nodded sympathetically.

Now there Tom lay, unbreathing, damaged, and stiff; no person, no soul, just the outward shell of a man, gothic, horrific, and accusatory. Cause of death, Chris Steiner explained, delicately indicating Tom Flynn's head with a silver pointer, was evidently suicide, as he would conjecture by the closeness of the firing range and the awkwardness of the bullet's angle of entry. The victim seemingly hesitated before firing, drawing the pistol away from his head before pulling the trigger. It was possible, of course, that he'd changed his mind at the last minute, with the gun going off accidentally: a hair trigger was typical of the .22 Luger found on the floor in Tom's office.

When Laureen brought out her camera, Steiner waved a no-no at her. Without pleading or objecting she put it away. In any event, she didn't feel she could photograph the corpse; rather, she marveled at Steiner's insouciance; but, then, he never knew the man and had no part in his death. This was his job. He had large pockets on his blue lab coat and carried his steel pointer the way a conductor might carry a baton. Death was his paycheck.

As she prepared to go, he asked her to leave his name out of any article she might write. This was, he explained, always the rule. He nodded, suggesting to her that he and Joe Fallon had understood each other in the past. She assured him that she understood both him and Fallon as well. She thanked him but had one question.

"How far away?"

Steiner looked quizzically.

"From his head," she qualified. "How far was the gun from his head?"

"Oh," said Steiner. "Not far. A few inches. No more than three or four."

She was about to say, "Are you sure, then, it was suicide?" But she sensed the answer would be yes. Somehow murder didn't have the same neat calculation. That was exactly one week and four days ago. She'd had a slight headache ever since. Today, Saturday, her head really ached, now in memory of Tom Flynn's corpse. She decided to go back to bed in spite of all the caffeine she'd imbibed. So she took two Excedrin P. M., lay down again, and fell asleep for two hours.

It was after one o'clock when she awoke, weary but less upset. She tried phoning Rodger at his office, but he didn't answer; so she left a message for him to call her. Things had gotten too complicated. She felt desperate for him. She didn't want him to run off and then be found in his office with a bullet in his brain.

She felt the Costa Rica urge again: to disappear, to escape from everything, as everything now disgusted her, including herself; on the other hand, she wanted vaguely to protect her husband; but in her confusion, still fatigued after a long nap, she had difficulty with an agenda. There were too many items, too much to feel for rather than think about; not only her husband, but Sandra, Tom, Arthur Weisskoff, and that business of missing money, seventeen million, stashed somewhere in the wide world. And the fifteen pages from the briefcase. Then there was Frank

Van Dam, who began to plague her with deep suspicion: him. He must've been involved in the Flamingo Affair. To rest her pulsing brain she decided to turn on the television, catch the news, and if not that then some stupid afternoon talk show. She didn't get to the talk show.

The newscaster on Channel 12 stood in front of an impressive house in a wooded area, a house resembling the Tudor grandeur of the Flynns' home; in fact, it was the Flynns' home. She recognized the yellow chrysanthemums in the window boxes. More time-filling palaver about Tom Flynn's suicide, she thought, lowering her eyelids and sitting back to listen. But that was not the subject. The pronouns kept coming up as "she"--she was the niece of former county political leader Arthur Weisskoff; she married Tom Flynn almost ten years ago; she . . . she . . . she--of course, the subject was Sandra. And then she heard the words: "bludgeoned to death late this morning in her home . . . ."

She grabbed the clicker to turn up the volume. She sat up, straightened her back, then stood leaning towards the television set. Say it again, say it again, she urged the newscaster, who suddenly returned the viewer to the pert, blonde, and perfectly coiffed Marsha Wilson sitting in the studio at the anchor's desk.

"A terrible and as yet unexplainable tragedy," was Marsha's comment before she switched to news about the sewage line blockage in Lindenhurst. Laureen clicked through all the other channels, then stopped in frustration. She turned off the television and dialed Rodger again at the office. No response. She phoned the secretary in the college's Criminal Justice Department: no response. It was

Saturday. The only one there might've been Rodger, who'd perhaps stepped out for minute; perhaps was on his way home.

She sat still, dazed by the news. This time she was part of it. She could gaze down at Tom Flynn and feel sick in a general way. The man was dead, and this was public information. She was part of that, too. But Sandra was not political, was not an item in her journalistic career. Sandra was Sandra. So she sat still, waiting for tears, waiting for a violence in her heart to break out. Nothing materialized except a vacant dullness.

"No, no," she murmured. "It's not right, not right."

She sat silently, stone still.

After forty minutes in a catatonic state, a surge of energy compelled her to find out more of this terrible, this insane news--driven, now, by the hysteria rising into her brain that her husband might be Sandra's killer. She got into her Toyota and drove, hoping to catch Rodger in his office. She needed desperately to know that her husband had been at his desk all day. He had to be, she kept repeating as she drove. And yet. If he'd been guilty in the cause of one death, well, what could he not be guilty of? And she, she, too, needed a friend; if he didn't bludgeon Sandra to death that morning, well, she needed Rodger to calm her down.

At the Social Science Building she used the back entrance, which she knew would be open for the maintenance crew. Breathlessly, she climbed two flights and came into the office area. Though all the ceiling lights were on, the place was empty. Rodger's door was open, and there, alone, was a fretful dark-skinned girl, evidently a student, sporting a floppy yellow cap and a surprisingly green overcoat with large lapels, staring out the window. Catching herself up, the girl turned to Laureen with a nervous smile.

"And you are?" asked Laureen.

"Takeesha," said the girl, "Takeesha . . . Montaigne. I'm a student of Prof. Metcalf's. They, they just took him away." She indicated the window.

Laureen moved swiftly towards the window and looked out, seeing only the security drive and nothing else.

"No," said Takeesha, "they're gone. They just drove away."

"Who?"

"The police." The girl's mouth was open, her eyes wide. "I'm so scared. For him." Her look said, "For me too." She continued, "I thought, at first, that I--." She stopped and stared at the older woman.

Laureen's worst expectation: Rodger arrested! There had to be some mistake; it was not possible, not true. Not serious, not serious, at all. He had to have been crazy to murder Sandra Flynn. But, of course, she remembered how he snarled out the word "lesbianism." Possibly, though, the police picked him up simply to discuss the case of Tom Flynn. Or had the authorities suddenly caught up with him for killing his former friend? After what he'd confessed to her, she wondered now if he could kill if the situation called for murder. Or perhaps the authorities needed a black scapegoat. To calm herself, she stepped back to cast a hard, rude look at this surprise female presence in her husband's office.

Takeesha had smooth deep bronze skin and watery dark brown eyes; though full in the breast with nice posture, she was not pretty. The girl stared back at her as if to question the meaning of the arrest as well as the appearance of this, to her, ill-mannered stranger. Those eyes stared, too, with a note of guilt, as the girl backed herself away from the window, her green coat open and flowing outward.

"I'm his wife," said Laureen. "You can tell me."

"Oh," said the girl, guiltier than ever. She slid over to the swivel chair used by her professor, and sat. "I'm sorry. I'm so sorry." Sorry for sitting? Her eyes, moving now from side to side, showed a desire for escape. Unnerved, she seemed ready to rise and make a dash for the door; Laureen, however, had blocked the way. So the girl sat still, her eyes moving, moving.

"Tell me everything," Laureen ordered.

"I'll try," replied Takeesha, looking down and away.

"Why was he arrested?"

"The murder," answered the girl: "At least something like murder. I think. I don't know. You know, the woman who was bludgeoned in Belvedere? Sandra Flynn, I think? It was on the news. Something to do with that, I think."

"You think."

"Everything happened so suddenly. They came and called him out of the office and then he went away with them. I'm so scared. I heard them talking really fast. I'm sorry. That's all I can tell you. I actually thought it was something that we'd, I mean, I'd, I mean, we'd . . . done." Stopping abruptly, she looked up at her professor's wife.

"Did Rodger, did Mr., I mean, did Prof. Metcalf say anything as this went on?"

The girl shook her head.

"He left without saying goodbye."

"And you, what were you doing here on a Saturday afternoon?"

"Nothing," Takeesha opened her eyes very wide, then looked quickly down. She glanced up from under her eyebrows. "Nothing at all . . . here. I came to him to talk about a paper I'd written. I had an appointment. He knew I had to be here for a rehearsal in the theater."

"At three o'clock on a Saturday afternoon?" How had this day had gone so wrong? Laureen felt dragged and spun about in a kind of delirium. Sandra's murder and now Rodger's arrest for it? An arrest? Or did this Takeesha get it mixed up? Was it for something innocent, traffic tickets, an unpaid fine? Surreal. And no escape from it. How would the police know where to find him? Had they checked at home first? And now this black girl, this Takeesha Montaigne, in her husband's office? And, yes, she corrected herself, this nubile co-ed, this almost homely though flamboyant young lady with her prominent breasts and floppy yellow cap and overwhelming green overcoat, who, sat there, embracing herself underneath those breasts and glancing slowly left and right at the floor, guilty as sin.

She repeated the question.

The girl shook her head; she took a deep breath. "I'm so scared." She looked straight up at Laureen. "I'm not a bad girl, Mrs. Metcalf."

"I didn't say you were," said Laureen, inhaling deeply. "You know best. You were with him today. And you may have gotten the facts wrong. Yes, I know a woman was murdered today. Some time this morning. Prof. Metcalf was probably here at that time grading papers. Of course, he may have been brought in for questioning regarding that crime. Being a criminal justice expert, he may have been required to offer a consultation. Then, again, it might've been nothing." She realized she offered the girl too much in the way of excuse. To set herself right, she said, "You seem to have been caught with him. Otherwise you wouldn't be so restless, so scared. Tell me everything about you and your professor. Tell me the truth." Mightn't she be Rodger's alibi? Some alibi. Laureen continued to breathe deeply: she had to clear her head for what she might hear next.

Takeesha put her hand to her open mouth and looked off. "What will happen if I tell you?" she asked.

"Nothing," said Laureen. "if you're innocent just tell me. You understand: this is serious."

Of all the damned things. A student was about to confess to an affair with her husband, here in his office. She wanted all the gory details, even as the sickness around her heart urged her to avoid the question. Not now, not ever, did she want to know again that her husband had abandoned her and taken up with a student. It was mere treachery, especially after the other night's hypocritical self-righteousness. For trampled on it was, that confession of hers. Stupidly, too. And all she'd thought about today was trying to keep him from the law! Her only thought today was his protection! She continued to force herself to breathe.

"I feel so guilty," the girl went on. She drew the side of her lower lip into her mouth.

"You're going to tell me everything."

"I don't think I can; I'm so . . . ashamed."

"Tell me."

"No, please. I don't want anyone to get into trouble. Not Prof. Metcalf or me. You know, I'm going to be in the school play. It's *As You Like It*; and I play Rosalind. I'm the lead. I don't, I don't want to lose the role, Mrs. Metcalf. And now seeing you, I'm sorry. I've been so careless." On the verge of tears, the girl wrung her hands. "But, actually, I might be proof of his innocence." She opened her eyes wide. "Maybe I can trust you?" The question sounded like a plea.

"Go ahead," offered Laureen. "Trust me. At least, I won't interfere with your career in the theater. Only consider: you might've been out with a murderer."

Takeesha shook her head and gazed at the floor. She sucked her lips in a few times, chewing on them. Then she straightened up, inhaled deeply, and spoke.

"I came into his office at one o'clock. He'd been waiting for me. We took a ride to the beach. We didn't have sex," she offered, "not exactly."

Laureen asked a few more questions. Her head was clearing. She kept her voice monotone. How wearisome. Yet in her reluctance to pounce, she must have seemed sympathetic; for the girl needed an audience, it seemed, being worried not only about losing her part in the play but, also, getting arrested for, what could it be, seducing a teacher or being an accomplice to a murder? An adult audience was like a visit to the confessional--and any adult could somehow possess the aura of a priest. Crazily, it might be a special dispensation for that adult to be also the "wife"; and a black one at that. It didn't hurt for the girl to be the same color, for if Laureen were white, the girl would not have been so ready to tell the story. So the wife put on her most neutral face. And then out came a detailed account of Rodger and Takeesha's day at Smith Point Beach.

"I've been stupid," the girl began, turning her eyes to the floor. "He told me that he thought black was beautiful. What a line. From a black teacher."

They'd parked in the vast, lonesome public lot at Smith Point about a hundred yards from the beach; that is, after they'd kissed in his office once they'd finished discussing her paper, on which she received an A. He said he needed to talk to someone, someone intelligent; someone who didn't need to understand, only listen and smile. She'd volunteered. He told her she had a sweet smile; and, for her part, she admitted to having a crush on him ever since the first day of the semester. And he'd always been a gentleman--always treated her as if she were special. Today was an awful day, overcast and cold, the kind of day that made her feel empty. It was so many hours before the rehearsal; and she'd pretty much learned her lines. So she agreed to go for a ride. It seemed exciting to go with him.

Once they parked, Rodger turned off the ignition and started talking about pheromones.

"Your body," he'd told her, as they sat together in the car, "gives off chemicals called pheromones. They're like an aroma from perfume or aftershave lotion. That's the reason we're attracted to each other. We can't help it. The effect is subconscious." He'd paused, gazing off in the distance. "I find you appealing," he continued, turning to look deeply into her eyes. "Those dark eyes," he said, "and you so pretty...."

"And so young," she added.

"So beautiful," he corrected her, as if she was his favorite beauty. "It's true. It's beauty that makes young and old irrelevant."

It was thrilling to hear that.

And then they moved closer, almost facing each other. Rodger pushed her green overcoat back from her shoulders. Twisting out of it, the girl sat in her blouse--a silky purple blouse: revealed as she illustrated the move to Laureen-- and let the coat crumble behind her in the seat. (Keeping that outlandish yellow cap on her head, thought Laureen.)

"The car was warm; the windows had fogged," Takeesha sucked her lips in, glancing away towards the window. "I took his hand and put it on my breast."

Then they kissed.

"I'm so sorry; I'm so sorry. It was wrong, and I knew it at the time," she went on. "But maybe there was something to what he said about pheromones, you know, that sometimes we can't help ourselves."

Tedious, hearing the girl plead her own innocence. Even so, Laureen was fascinated by the details while loathing them: not shocked, though, as this sort of thing had happened before, and he'd confessed and made promises. Some promises. She had never felt entirely secure with the man, not in the romantic sense; but she'd always been able to talk to him, to rely on his sympathy, his friendship. She attributed his irresponsible behavior, his shallowness, as she explained him to herself, to some mysterious trauma in past--perhaps the very thing he revealed to her two nights ago. And if so, why such blatant treachery today, this day, with Takeesha Montaigne? Oh, there was more to know. Really, it seemed, his outpouring of that rainy night and then his anger at her two nights ago simply opened up the gates of desire, compelling him to run free with anyone anywhere. Or did it lead to violence: had her husband killed Sandra this morning and then gone off with this college slut in the afternoon? Too bizarre.

Laureen, who'd removed her coat and sat in the other chair in the office, breathed slowly through her nostrils. She was clear now, professional. She knew that she must've been born to listen to people; this was how she made a career in journalism. Yet how painful this could be--and how ironic that she never lost her appetite for information, even as it injured her self-esteem. And here was Takeesha--love that name, she said to herself--whose main object, apparently, was to exonerate herself in confession, to relieve herself of pain, as if the wife were not so much wife as priest--or maybe just girlfriend. She had this effect on nearly everyone, this evocative force, that in the process, ironically, canceled out her own personality.

"Do you understand who you're speaking to?" she asked the girl, dropping and folding her hands on her lap.

"I know you're a reporter. Rodger, Prof. Metcalf, told me about you, that you might win a Pulitzer Prize," the girl answered guilelessly. "I guess you could write this all up in the newspaper, if you wanted to; but now that you've got me here, I think I need to be honest. I'll never see him again. I promise."

Laureen nodded, almost smiling. "Probably not," she said. And then to herself: possibly neither will I.

"I should tell you, though, that he told me all about the Flamingo Affair," the girl added.

Realizing the office door had been open all this time, Laureen rose and shut it. She came and sat again opposite the girl. She saw that Ms. Montaigne was young, no more than eighteen or nineteen, but in listening to her gathered that she was not particularly stupid. Ms. Montaigne was handling the situation as best she could.

"The Flamingo Affair," Laureen stated calmly.

"You know," nodded the girl, "when the politician died. Something like ten years ago."

"Yes, I remember."

"He seemed to feel guilty about it."

"Really."

"Maybe you already know."

Laureen shook her head slowly. "Not everything."

"Not everything from today," Takeesha came near to smiling and, sensing that the professor's wife was not going to have her arrested or kicked out of school, went on to tell of her and Rodger's walk on the beach.

"Afterwards"--apparently some sort of sex had occurred in the car--"Rodger wanted to explore the beach. He'd felt faint."

They walked across the parking lot and through the tunnel under the boardwalk to the beach. It was bleak there, but Takeesha went along even though she feared it might rain, for the wind had become blustery. Luckily, it didn't rain; so they walked and walked past the boardwalk (holding hands, Laureen imagined) on the undulations of the damp tan beach. The sea was foamy with dark green billows crashing on the sand, so they hewed to the upper part of the beach, where they spied an old rowboat run ashore. Oh, look, she'd cried, pointing to the wreck. It lay half-submerged in sand below the irregular faded-red pickets of the wooden storm fence hedging in the dunes. She broke from Rodger, running toward the gray, weathered thing--just a rowboat, its bottom eroded, filled with sand. He followed. They found an old oar there, broken off halfway up the stem. When she went to grab the paddle at the bottom, Rodger pulled her back, saying, no, don't, please.

She looked back at him, annoyed. But he turned away from her and then suddenly fell to his knees, holding his head in his hands. She tried to find out the matter, but he only shook his head. Then he rose, brushed himself off, and walked ahead of her, back across the beach, through the tunnel under the boardwalk leading to the parking lot, and then into the car.

He didn't speak much, if at all.

They came back to the campus--where that evening she had to go to a rehearsal in the theater.

There were things Laureen wanted to say, but her nose started to run again. Her head felt heavy, and tears blurred her vision. The cold had returned, and she was beside herself for relief. The girl, standing, about to leave, handed her the box of Kleenex from Rodger's desk. Laureen accepted it, nodding.

"Mind if I go?" the girl asked.

Preoccupied, the professor's wife waved her away with the back of her hand.

"Oh," said the girl, turning at the door, "That woman who was killed, Sandra Flynn? That was Tom Flynn's, that politician's, wife?"

"Yes," was all Laureen could answer.

"I don't know," said Takeesha. "It's what got me thinking when you mentioned it just now. When we drove away to the beach, we heard on the car radio that she'd been killed, and his whole mood got really scary. Prof. Metcalf began to shake his head crazy-like but wouldn't explain why. I didn't think much of it, because as we parked, he settled down and got very sexy . . . and so I got sexy too. I never realized that he could have been involved."

"Figures," Laureen nodded. Tears streamed down her face. She blew her nose for the sixth or seventh time.

"Maybe he just knew her."

"Maybe."

"Very sad," offered the girl. "But will the police...?"

"Maybe not," said Laureen.

Pensively, Takeesha turned to go.

"Oh," she turned back again. "I remember. The teacher who's directing the school play told me he knows you."

This sex thing of her husband's had bandied her name about with another teacher? Laureen directed a fierce look at Takeesha, who faced her with idiotic innocence.

"Sonny."

"Sonny?"

"Sonny Anzalone. He's a professor in the Theater Department. He's directing me in *As You Like It*, by Shakespeare. Somehow during a party with the cast, some of them were talking about the election, and your name came up. And I said I had her husband as my Criminal Justice professor. And Sonny laughed and said he knew you when."

"Really."

The girl left, smiling and nodding.

Laureen sat at Rodger's desk, preparing to speak all she'd heard from Takeesha into her digital recorder. At the moment she failed to put anything together; so she sat, blew her nose, and wiped her eyes. It was astonishing how many emotions went through a person's head and how much wetness could ooze out of a person's eyes and nose. Then, again, what did anything matter? Was Sandra really dead? Had she been murdered? And was Sandra's death worse than her husband's senseless betrayal? And had that death really anything to do with Rodger earlier in the day? She blew her nose again. Had she, Laureen, been so bad a human being that she should suffer these losses so suddenly after enjoying the glory of the election returns and the promise of a Pulitzer? But now what actually seemed worst of all was the reflection that talk got around so easily and so shabbily. Had the student cast of *As You Like It* heard Sonny Anzalone announce that he knew her when?

She stood, shaking her head slowly; she snatched a mass of tissue from the Kleenex box; then she grabbed her black overcoat and purse. Numbly, she walked out of the office, shutting the light and making sure the door was locked behind her. She proceeded down the back stairs and outside into the rear parking lot. Halfway to her car, she halted, not knowing where to go or what to do next. The area was dark, desolate; the parking lot lights were on, revealing the emptiness of the place, the stillness of the building, the meaninglessness of everything. The sky was dark, covered with a layer of cloud. She felt obscure, helpless. She looked for Rodger's maroon Buick but saw nothing. He might have driven it himself, following the police. On the other hand, it might've been impounded.

Her worst expectations had come true. In all ways. And aside from her clothes, the girl herself was nothing to look at.

Weary, overwhelmed, she hardly knew where to turn. All of life seemed bothersome.

She needed to go somewhere.

It occurred to her to drive over to the Liberal Arts Building and see this Sonny, someone she hadn't had contact with in many years, not since she'd married Rodger. Sonny, she recalled, was a bit irregular but always friendly: and, desperately she told herself, any port in a storm. So, after driving across campus, she parked and walked into the back of the building and down the long hallway to the theater office.

CHAPTER SEVEN
Flamingo Desires

Hearing her own footsteps in the hallway, she glanced around for anyone who might be in the rooms to left and right. No one. She checked her watch: six o'clock. There would be a rehearsal, but she didn't know when; should she go back to her car? No, here was Sonny in his office next to the entrance of the theater, scribbling at his desk--leaping up absolutely gleeful as he noticed her. He embraced her, kissing her on both cheeks and telling her not to worry, they had plenty of time before the kids arrived. There would be only two of them, students: Takeesha, who played Rosalind, and another girl, who played Celia. "Just some work on character relationships; won't last more than an hour. Stick around." He took her overcoat and tossed it on a chair. Then he offered her a drink from a sterling silver cocktail shaker in his little fridge: a Manhattan. Incongruous as the drink was, the receptacle he poured it into, a Styrofoam cup, made her laugh. So did the maraschino cherry he plopped into it.

Sonny had been part of the gay crowd from Sayville way back when. They'd meet at parties from time to time; they got to like each other. "And then you were married," said Sonny. "Heavens." She noticed his increased weight along with his round bald spot: from which, like a monk's, his hair crept away on all sides. "Go ahead, look," he said. "Fat and forty; actually, fat and forty-four. But you, you look fabulous; well, you'd look fabulous if you didn't have such a red nose and all that snot coming out of it."

She laughed, gulped down the Manhattan, then had to blow her nose several times. She asked him if he'd heard the news about Sandra; he said he had. She told him that she'd seen the dead woman only yesterday. He said he hadn't seen her in many moons. But he, too, was full of grief, and that is why she caught him drinking all this hard stuff.

"You don't imagine I do this before every rehearsal, do you?"

Actually, she did.

"Usually afterwards. They don't pay me enough to go sipping this stuff in a bar."

She needed to know where he got his crushed ice. He jabbed a thumb toward his little fridge alongside the far end of his desk. It had a freezer compartment "for the purpose"; and then, going to the appliance again, he offered her some cheese, which he placed on a paper plate and sliced with a knife from his top drawer; then he came up with a tin of crackers. So they munched and talked.

"You cast a black girl in the lead of *As You Like It*?" Laureen asked.

"Sure," said Sonny. "It's done all over. No difference in race, not in the theater."

"Really." She felt moved by this, more than she expected. But the conversation changed direction.

She mentioned about Takeesha's being Rodger's student and meeting him on campus earlier, then disappearing with him. She left out the beach-scene but said something about the subsequent police visit and Rodger's being called in to the precinct house. By now she couldn't remember if handcuffs played a role in the call--or if it had been only a consultation. Her husband, perhaps, merely offered his help as a criminal expert. True, he may have bludgeoned

Sandra Flynn to death. She didn't say that out loud, but her look suggested something criminal about Rodger; and for her to reveal that made her realize that she'd become quickly drunk.

"Exciting," commented Sonny casually. "But farfetched. If I committed a violent homicide in the morning, I'd be home right now totally plastered. I wouldn't have come to school to discuss research papers with my students."

"Yes, but . . . ."

"It's nothing," he assured her. "Stop worrying; keep drinking."

They meandered into the past, reminiscing about Sandra and her amusing ways.

After her third cocktail Laureen became quiet. So Sonny began to speak about his concerns, launching into production issues as if life had now become a total abstraction and the only tangible reality existed in the theater.

The main problem with Takeesha's character, Sonny explained, was that as Rosalind in *As You Like It* she needed to spend most of the play impersonating a boy. "Can you imagine?" With his hands he fashioned breasts and hips. "Such a girl. Still, she has talent. Anyway, that was part of the practice tonight. But what the hell, tonight we need to cry on each other's shoulder. Let's forget about Takeesha and Rodger and everyone else in this bizarre excuse for a world. I'll tell those two young ones to go home." Which is what he did at seven o'clock. Laureen couldn't care less. The two of them, Sonny and she, continued to drink.

"She's disgusting," said the professor's wife.

"Not at all," the other replied.

Is so, she said to herself; and what would Sonny know about whether or not a girl was attractive or disgusting or whatever? Had he heard somewhere that full breasts made a woman beautiful? Is that why he chose Takeesha as his female lead? The one who'd need help in playing a boy?

She jumped to another, related topic. Sexual confusion, she contended out loud, was something Sonny seemed to be good at. Out of focus, she'd meant to be complimentary, but she sounded so clumsy formulating the idea that it came off wrong. "I'm not a transvestite," he defended himself; on the other hand, he was far from offended but, rather, challenged. "Let me show you the costumes," he suggested.

"Please, do," she said, pleasantly and demonstratively awe-struck as he managed to mix up his delicious Manhattans, as if out of nowhere. "Because I think you're amazing." He had charm, this Sonny; he had warmth; he had flair. For the moment he was what she needed.

"I think so too," he agreed, pouring out her fourth drink. Then he led her into the costume room, a deep, dark chamber, peopled by dummies and filled towards the rear with volumes of clothing on racks. One florescent light shone over a clean, pine-top cutting table, upon which Sonny lifted his bulk, sitting with hands holding the thick edge. "You're not spooked by all this, are you?" he asked. She shook her head. "Because there are ghosts back there," he gestured to the shadowy area of the clothing racks. "The students have seen them. I've seen one once." He paused for a reaction; Laureen offered none. The room took on a glamorous iridescence, as she noted that the light from above, white as it was, glanced off all the mirrors and metal in the room. "Go ahead," Sonny offered; "try something on." He stretched his hand back into the darkness. "Something masculine. See how well you do."

She stepped curiously into the darkness, finding a tuxedo jacket and top hat. She came back wearing them, sauntering with a man-like stride and standing before him with her head to one side.

"Not bad, Butch," he said. "The costume flatters you; and vice-versa. Could you give a soulful blues version of 'Lili Marlene'?"

Agreeably, she proceeded to give a throaty rendition of "Falling in Love Again" in what she imagined was à la Eartha Kitt with a German accent: "Falling in luf again, vhat could I do? Never vanted to, cahn't help it."

"This is as far as I go," she said.

"Don't we all know," he said gently.

"Oh, what do you know," she sighed; "you know nothing."

"I know who loved you," he replied. "And maybe who you loved in return."

"No, not enough," she said. "And enough of that." The truth, to her in her drunkenness, was that Sandra's death, sudden and awful as it was, left her ambivalent: devastated but relieved. It took four Manhattans for her to reach down inside herself to see that. But also to wonder why she, black as she was, always felt invisible, overlooked, hidden. Was she the cause of her own obscurity? Drunk as she was, she found no answer. Sonny must've read a strangeness in her expression as she related this to herself, because he laughed gaily and told her that instead of needling her with foolish commentary he would tell her of his encounter with love as a young man, something, if she could believe him, he'd never told anyone.

"I visited Las Vegas," he began, staring off as the scene grew vivid in his imagination. He was seventeen, flying with his Uncle Mario to Nevada. The man had been promised a job in a casino out there. They stayed at the original Flamingo, built in the 1940s by Bugsy Siegel, the notorious, gunned-down gangster. There he saw glamorously costumed, long-legged, gum-chewing, chorus-line lovelies, he chatted with hoodlums in tuxedos, and he got to shake hands with a pudgy-faced Wayne Newton at the start of his long Las Vegas career. Back then it was exciting. "Today there's still sex galore, but the fancy tough guys are all gone," he sighed, "and everyone wears horrendous t-shirts and baggy Bermuda shorts." He continued, mixing fact with fiction, describing the newer, larger, and more glittery Flamingo with its palm-tree-lined pool and impressive memorial niche, festooned, as he said, with vines and blossoms: a monument dedicated to the ill-fated thug who made Las Vegas happen. There it was, on a high rectangular base: a plaque with the gangster's face engraved on it. The face was surrounded by a wheel of fortune, and on that wheel was an inscription that read: "Bugsy Siegel died for your spins."

Once she understood what he said, Laureen began laughing hysterically.

"It's true," he insisted.

"No, it's not," she said, stopping. "You've used that line before."

"Maybe once or twice," he allowed. "But only in church: it's so theological. But let's get back to me. While at the old Flamingo I met a young gentleman traveling with his uncle, a gambler. And there we gambled also, in a lovelier way, not with chips but with ourselves. And there, guilty as sin, we discovered . . . ourselves." He opened his eyes wide, raising his eyebrows.

"Was that the beginning of a long, passionate, and frustrating love affair?" she asked.

He closed his eyes briefly. "Not at all. Suddenly, it was over before it started. A crapshoot, you could say, where I lost what I'd won. Even worse, my uncle never took the job. What about you? What's your latest perversion?"

"After having brought Tom Flynn to ruin and tragic death?"

"Really," Sonny rolled his eyes.

"After losing someone I did love once, I confess it, in a horrible murder?"

"I'm so sorry, Laureen."

"The list goes on. Now let's really consider this. I need to hear your entire take on it? About Rosalind, the one in your newest production, that calypso Lolita, that young, nubile thing who just spent the afternoon at the beach giving my husband a blow job." She paused.

"This afternoon?" questioned Sonny, visibly shocked.

"Isn't that what I said?" Hadn't she said that several times already? Hadn't it been buzzing through her head all the time she been talking to Sonny?

"Well, it seems so recent."

"Would it be any better if it happened last week?"

"No, not at all. But at least you and I would have had time to get used to the idea. A blow job at the beach? Today? Disgusting!" He waited a beat. "I wish I'd been there."

"Shut up," she said. "These co-eds are game for any kind of sex. Why else do they come to college? They should be offered course-credit in Intro to Illicit Casual Sex. Just to get them to feel a little guilty and then to keep them from becoming totally diseased." Then she started giggling, thinking about how the school paper could advertise for such encounters; "No, listen: Applications for Fellatioship in Crime Study."

Sonny smiled, then soberly insisted that she wasn't all that funny.

Realizing how drunk she was and how the conversation had deteriorated, she assumed an air of dignity. "That ends my marriage."

The two of them sat, as Laureen had jumped up on another cutting table facing Sonny, and gazed downward, glumly.

"Not the first time?" Sonny said, not looking up.

"No."

"That calls for another," he said, slipping down and walking away. "Be right back."

She wanted to collapse in tears on the floor, but something held her back: "No meaning," she said out loud; "what a pity." She was not a weeper anyway. Alone in this chamber of costumes, this fantasy world of might-be-could-be, she slid off the cutting table and turned to peer back into the darkness. She had no reason to cry, being totally soggy-headed. This is what happens when you drink too much: can't feel, can't cry, she said to herself. She removed the top hat and black jacket and tossed them on the table. She felt a shrewd chill, then a spasm of fear. She seemed to see a movement in the darkness at the rear. She remembered that Sonny spoke of students seeing ghosts there; that he himself had seen one once. She didn't believe in dead spirits who visited the living--and yet she sensed for a second a flutter among the hanging fabrics, chiaroscuroed in the dim florescence. Again, that spasm of fear thrilled her body. She wanted to run, but she stood stuck to the spot and instead called loudly, almost hysterically, "Sonny! Sonny! Sonny!"

He appeared, sterling silver cocktail shaker in hand, "Could you do that a little louder? Nobody can hear you in the other buildings on campus." He filled her Styrofoam cup, adding the cherry. "You look like you've seen a ghost."

"No," she said. "I just got scared."

"Happens to me all the time. Guilt. For all the things that I did that I shouldn't have and vice-versa. That's why I drink. *Salute*." They touched cups.

"Sex," she toasted. "Can't live with it, and can't live with it."

"Is that deep?" he questioned. "If not, it ought to be. They should make laws," he continued, "about emotional depth. Speaking of which," he picked up again, "you shouldn't feel guilty about Tom Flynn. I know more things about him than you'd suspect."

"From whom?" she asked.

"From a mutual friend, whom I may or may not introduce to you, if I can ever get him to start talking to me again."

"That would be interesting," Laureen nodded, sensing that she'd begun to slow her speech while slurring a few words. "Anyone else you know something about?"

"Yes," he answered. "His wife."

"Sandra?"

"Didn't you know that she and I . . . oh, I can't go into it. It would be inappropriate, given the events of the day."

"So . . . what?" she uttered slowly, heavily.

"Okay, I will. One night. We did something foolish. Right here in this costume room."

As the tale unfolded--though who could believe any of it, coming from Sonny--Sandra had sought him out late one afternoon many years back after she'd heard that Tom Flynn had a boyfriend, someone he'd met during the Flamingo Affair and who now worked at the college. She'd come to confront the guy, only to be detoured into Sonny's realm of the theater, where she, as now Laureen, wound up drinking with him into the wee small hours.

"You mean to tell me that Tom Flynn was gay?" Laureen asked, incredulous; her jaw hung slack and her head moved from side to side.

"Bi. Fatally bi. Like so many others," shrugged Sonny, sighing.

"I'll be damned," she said.

"Oh, you already are," he added, "like so many others."

He went on to describe a hideously comical scene that ensued as Sandra and he got drunker and drunker.

"Apropos of our discussion of confused sexuality," Sonny sounded almost sober as he began, "Sandra wanted me to suppose that for a moment she was a man. She wore a man's suit from off the rack back there and a man's fedora. In fact, what happened with you tonight was, for me, a bit of déjà vu. But Sandra strutted around with her elbows out and her hips square--most convincingly. I'd be lucky if I could do as well. This, you know, is what I'm teaching Takeesha to do as Rosalind. I learned it all from Sandra. But getting back . . . .

"Everyone knows that sexual attraction is an illusion," he continued, "and in the grip of that illusion, in a fleeting moment--Sandra wanted to know if I could take her like a boy.

" 'For a boy?' I asked.

" 'No, like a boy,'" she insisted.

"I laughed. 'Sandra,' I asked, 'are you making a pass at me?' She nodded yes. 'Are you crazy?' I said.

" 'Yes,' she answered, 'and drunk and pissed and ready for anything.' She cursed Tom and his boyfriend (who is actually quite a nice guy and who was once a close personal friend of mine whom I may introduce to you) and claimed that if they could engage in desperate sex so could she. Then I remember almost word for word what she spoke:

" 'Let's say,' she said, 'that I am totally unreal. Finally, everything is unreal, isn't it? And this is the theater, where everyone finds truth in their illusions. Where we become what it is possible to become. So imagine, Sonny, that I am not what I am. Imagine, instead, that I am, for a fleeting moment, someone else.' Who did she have in mind? 'That boy, for instance, in Las Vegas at the original Flamingo.'

" 'This is all very seductive,' I replied--and, yes, she was the other person I told my story to. I wanted to slip away from her, but I didn't. 'All very seductive,' I said, 'but I have a more vivid memory of the Nevada desert that I do of that boy. Everyone leaves himself behind somewhere; everything after is an alibi.' " he added. Then he continued, playing both parts, his and Sandra's.

" 'Then find the truth in me,' she said. She reached out to me with both hands, caressing my chest and arms. Her eyes--you remember her green, green eyes--they glittered here in the darkness as if she was possessed.

" 'Why?' I questioned.

" 'To help me,' she said simply. 'I need love. Or a reasonable facsimile.'

"I honestly did my best to say no," Sonny continued, "but somehow she was irresistible.

"She pressed against me, looking up at me with those fascinating, seductive eyes. 'I think you're beautiful, Sonny,' she whispered lusciously. "Your face is so sweet, so sweet, like a woman's. Let me kiss you: your lips are so round and full. Your eyes are dreamy, a dreamy, dreamy blue; I adore those long dark lashes. If I were a boy, I'd find you sexy.' So then she kissed me. I tried to break away, but suddenly she seemed to have the strength of two people, since she was at that moment both a man and a woman.

" 'Go,' I said, though, I admit, very weakly. 'Go away.'

" 'Okay,' she answered in a deep, resonant baritone, 'I'll leave. But think, Sonny: This is one of those special moments when that other part of you--the dark side of your mystery--might find itself fulfilled. One of those moments when you might discover an intense, fleeting beauty. When flamingo desires seem real and graspable. Kiss me.'

"So I did. And in the twinkling of an eye there I was, Homo erectus. Unabashedly man-like, and in the twinkling of an eye I took her like a boy. My god. The surprising moment of primeval memory."

He smiled a weird, flabby smile.

"My god," echoed Laureen; and then began weeping. She couldn't stop.

Soon she lost consciousness. She opened her eyes again in Sonny's car as he drove her back to Brentwood. Groggily, she thanked him. She went inside and fell asleep in the den on the tan leather couch. Instead of a blanket, she wore the black overcoat that Sonny dressed her in when she found herself lost from within.

CHAPTER EIGHT
Smith & Wesson

She dreamed of her old high school, walking through the hall invisibly as the other students passed her by. She was lonely, afraid. No one could see her, even as she greeted her old friends, both boys and girls. The period bell began to ring; she tried to get to class but couldn't find the door. No one would tell her where she should go. She panicked, tried to run, but went nowhere. Sandra appeared then: she was only a face, a face that reached to kiss her. When Laureen moved to take the kiss, she found the face without substance, only an image. It was then that she could hear herself scream and scream again.

She awoke without a doubt that Frank Van Dam had been her source all along for the information that would indict Tom Flynn.

But that was not all.

"VD," she repeated to herself as if in a trance, "VD." She remembered that in high school she'd associated his name with venereal disease. "But I'd forgotten," she whispered.

Odd, almost mystical, this connection. But there was basis for it.

She sat up in bed, remembering scene after scene of twenty years back.

They were seniors in high school. That fall he'd been elected Class President. In the spring Laureen had been thrilled when he asked her to go off alone with him, separating from the group they'd hung with all year and in which she felt anonymous. As a white boy he was more than just friendly, and as a black girl she was cautious but more than flattered. He'd spoken of their going to the

Senior Prom together. It was night in a warm early May when they drove out east to a deserted beach between East Hampton and Montauk. Quiet except for the sound of the waves lapping lazily against the sandy shoreline, the setting was perfect for romance, the air sea-scented with a mix of salt and honey, the moonless sky filled with stars. He'd brought a blanket with him and laid it out on the sand. Soon they were clutching and kissing each other with delirious abandon. She let his hands roam over her body, over her breasts, then up her leg, then onto her belly, then under her belt-line and into her panties. Suddenly she'd wanted him to stop; it was going too far; she wasn't ready for him, not tonight. It all felt good, but it was too much, and she wanted him to stop. Yet he persisted. Soon her shoes were off, then her jeans, tossed on the sand beside the blanket; then her panties. She grew frightened, angry. She tried to push him away, but he was stronger. She tried to utter, "No, no, no," but the words stuck in her throat. Then she went blank.

From that point on she remembered nothing. When she came to, she was sitting in his car, feeling wet and sticky, her panties awkwardly fitted, her jeans draped over her lap. Frank was driving back to her house in North Shirley. She smelled of salt water; and when she asked him, he told her that, no, she hadn't fainted; she'd gone spookily quiet and helpless; so that he'd led her to the ocean, washed her, and then dressed her himself. He was nervous and shaky, smoking one cigarette after another. She was numb, dazed, stupidly trying to figure what had happened.

Afterwards he avoided her. She told herself it was back to being anonymous again; and at the same time she began to worry about contracting herpes or gonorrhea or, even worse, HIV. The worrying continued for months. Nothing occurred. Then a girlfriend, a white girl, told her that Frank was never going to take her to the Senior Prom. The girl told her that he didn't want to seem serious about a black girl. In the upshot, she didn't attend; and Frank took someone else. And what else was it but race?

She'd pushed it all down, out of awareness. From pride. From desperation. It was only now after the alcohol-induced nightmare, twenty years later, that she sensed the rape, felt his penetration and her unwilling acquiescence . . . and her fretting, fretting . . . and her deep sense of fear and disgust.

She knew now, as well, that Frank Van Dam was Sandra's killer.

The revelation ran through her brain only after her going from screaming in her dream to weeping awake hysterically for twenty minutes. Now it was after four in the morning. She'd been sleeping on the den couch in her clothes from last night. Weary, heavy in the head, she rose, went up to her bedroom, undressed, and fell onto her sheets only to think in a restless, groggy half-sleep for the next five hours. She awoke at nine. The phone had been ringing.

Drowsily, she picked up the receiver. It was Sonny. He asked if she was all right. He apologized for taking her home last night but told her that it was either that or have her sleep on the cutting table in the costume room. Her Toyota Camry was still in the parking lot near the Liberal Arts Building; and naturally Sonny would come over and give her a ride to fetch it.

The phone rang again. It was Fallon at the newspaper. He wondered why she hadn't sent any copy on Sandra Flynn's death. What, was she sleepwalking, he asked. You guessed it, she answered and hung up.

Her head didn't ache, but she was numb, depressed; she stared out the kitchen window onto her backyard--another bleak day with unraked leaves scattered on the grass. With an effort, she faced the reality of Sandra's death, the truth of which she'd drowned for a few hours with Sonny and his Manhattans. There'd be no more of those. She could cope with Sandra's death. It had been a long time since the two of them were friends. That vision of Sandra's face may have been Sandra's ghost bidding her goodbye. No, Laureen didn't believe in ghosts. Even so, she felt a dull ache in her heart, knowing, too, that that would pass; and probably that little party with Sonny last night was not such a bad thing.

Again she felt the prompting she'd felt in the dream but couldn't verbalize: Frank Van Dam was the perpetrator, the murderer. There it was: she'd solved the crime. Rodger was innocent; Van Dam, guilty. It was only for the police to arrest him. If only they could make the same connection she did. She needed to think. She could give up on her husband after his behavior yesterday; but not yet, not when, as she knew in her heart of hearts, Frank Van Dam was the one to get. But just accuse the man on the basis of a dream, a post-mortem dream? She would have to prove his guilt. It was impossible to retreat, to believe, naively, that the police would find the murderer as a matter of course. She understood that murders like Sandra's go unsolved--that black folks like Rodger Metcalf go to prison for what they didn't do. She'd done her job writing those articles for the newspaper, but there was more for her to do. There were larger issues here. She needed to think.

And where was that briefcase, those telling pages?

She remembered: no mail on Sunday. Tomorrow was Monday.

She sniffed at the air, and already, it seemed, her nose-cold was almost over.

Nauseous now, she walked head first hastily to the bathroom. There she began to vomit her guts out. Afterwards she felt relieved, fresher, but the mess had to be cleaned up, and then she needed a shower. Her husband, she noted as she returned to her bedroom, hadn't come home last night and then, in the shower, she visualized clearly, with heart beating and head aching after the vomit, how he'd gone off with the police, apparently in his own car. Still, less numb in the brain, she managed to dress herself in baggy jeans and sweatshirt, while questions spun around her skull. There was no actual arrest, was there? Certainly he didn't spend the night in the lock-up, did he? More likely, he--and here she remembered quite enough-- he felt too guilty to face her with his latest co-ed escapade. (Were they all as plain as Takeesha? as big-breasted?) But, then, how would he have known that she knew? The bastard. The miserable, self-righteous, sneaky em-effing (she used only initials) sonofabitch. She wanted to use more bad language, but she stopped after calling him a pervert out loud. Laureen saw that she needed to phone the police to find out if he was still with them or somewhere else. Once those papers arrived, she would save him in spite of himself. Then she'd divorce him. That would serve him right, this cruddy low-life she had the misfortune to marry.

Reconsidering, she decided to wait to phone the police. It was early. It was Sunday. She hardly cared if Rodger spent the night in the lock-up. She'd given him everything, and he'd given her nothing. That wasn't exactly true, but it suited her to think so. She dreaded answering the question of what was left for her. Then she sat sipping her three cups of coffee, thinking, thinking as she waited for Sonny to pick her up.

Rodger was a distraction she could've done without. There was Frank Van Dam and whether or not he was also implicated in Tom Flynn's "suicide." She put the word in quotation marks, sensing that there was a connection between the husband-and-wife deaths, maybe even an obvious one. If only she knew where to go with that. If Van Dam had killed Sandra, it might be sensible to begin with the motive. The briefcase, the diary?

She needed a friend, a supportive embrace, a leaning post, a rock. She sighed her way back to Rodger. Her thoughts swung back and forth. Perhaps her husband really had been brought in for questioning in the case of Sandra Flynn's being bludgeoned to death! The possibility had hovered over the previous afternoon and evening; but, seriously--and here was a back-swing--much as she felt hurt by the man, she knew he was innocent, simply by reason of his being a gutless sneak. So that now if he'd be arrested on that charge, she would have to get Takeesha Montaigne to provide the alibi. Yet establishing the alibi might lead to another problem. He could be fired on a morals charge.

Panicking, she reviewed the previous day. He'd gotten up and left the house early. She failed to reach him on the phone all morning and afternoon. Late in the day the police came to his office and escorted him out. Her mind spun. She tried to rein herself in, thinking, "People get brought into the police station for all sorts of reasons; rarely for murder." He had no motive for killing Sandra Flynn besides the fact that he'd always hated her. That was bad. But, actually, he'd spent the morning at school and the rest of the day with Takeesha Montaigne. No, she told herself: the culprit was Frank Van Dam; stick with him and make sure that dope Rodger stays off the hook.

Still curious, she dialed the number of the Fourth Precinct only to get a recorded announcement for her to leave a message. It was Sunday. Neither of the desk sergeants, Phil Coletti or Bob Mazell, her usual contacts, would be in. It was Sunday, the day after all the weekend bad stuff happened, and the precinct house would be a scene of incoherent noise, shuffling around, and general confusion. She dialed 911 but was told that unless there was an emergency she had to contact the police station to have her questions answered.

At least she had Sonny Anzalone: her rock. She considered telling him about her dream and then revealing to him all she knew about the leather briefcase and its presumed contents.

By now Sonny had arrived, and off they went to the Fourth Precinct on Veterans Highway in Hauppauge, where they were told that there was no file on Rodger Metcalf but that someone, possibly, at the Sixth Precinct in Coram, since that was the jurisdiction of the Flynn murder, might be able to offer more information. Possibly. Nothing could be clarified. On what charge? No charge, as far as they could say.

Off they went to the Sixth Precinct, where they were met with imperturbable blankness.

"Wow," said Sonny. "Pretty exciting, eh?"

She didn't answer: knowing nothing was not exciting.

"Totally in the dark," Sonny added, smiling weirdly.

Laureen had no recollection of Sonny's appearance last night, but today she found him in a state of gay flamboyance, blousy in his pineapple-colored flare-collared satin shirt with dark purple neckerchief, over which he wore a cream-colored cashmere coat knotted on his bulging waist with a matching buckle-less cashmere belt. His hair, in a self-conscious style, was combed over the top with a little upswing above his forehead. The bald spot persisted but less visibly. He glided as he walked.

"Exciting, I guess. For those of us without guilt," she commented.

"I never made that claim," he said. "But wasn't that Frank Van Dam in there?"

"Where?"

"Talking to someone, gesticulating wildly."

"Where?"

"In the office, to our right. I was sure you noticed him."

"I didn't."

"Should we go back in?" Sonny seemed eager for a scene.

"No," Laureen, with a shiver of fear, shook her head. She fretted that she might blurt out something stupid. Beyond that, she couldn't imagine what they might have said to each other. She burned, though, to know what Van Dam might want from the police. Put it aside, she told herself. She would have her moment with him, as she hoped.

They returned to Sonny's black-and-white Mini Cooper, an incongruously diminutive vehicle for such a bulky man. Laureen contemplated the drama of a potential meeting with the suave killer, the moment of truth with Frank Van Dam. With the briefcase papers in her hand and perhaps one necessary witness, just one.

As she speculated, Sonny began to ramble about his production of *As You Like It*. He couldn't, she considered, make much of a witness to anything. She ruminated on how much truth there was in Sonny's tale of sexual perversity with Sandra in the costume room. About to question him about it, she saw how futile that would be, since Sonny could either affirm or deny it as he saw fit, only to please the circumstance. She'd be left to feel more insecure than ever. Some of those lines he attributed to her seemed more like Sonny than Sandra. Yet it all seemed possible, knowing Sandra and her kookiness. She'd confessed to Laureen that she'd gone in for sex toys and group fun, something this girl, as she called herself, could never tolerate. But a night with Sonny?

As for Sonny's lack of reliability, she reasoned that all things were possible for all men and all women. Nobody had a center, a steady view of self. Self was only a philosophical speculation; and reality no better.

Through all this thinking, Laureen kept picturing Frank Van Dam, he in the precinct house in the office to her right, gesticulating wildly.

"Oh," said Sonny once they were a mile along the road toward the college, "while you were talking to the desk sergeant, I got a quick call on my cell phone, which you might've noticed. A friend of mine, someone I mentioned to you yesterday, wanted to come by my place for a brief visit. A very interesting friend. You might want to meet him."

"Why?"

"Just because."

"You were on the phone for about ten seconds."

"All he said was yes."

"You invited him before?"

"Yes."

They drove on William Floyd Parkway toward the college while going south to the Long Island Expressway. As the entrance gate was shut, it being Sunday, they would've had to spend another half hour contacting the guard house, waiting for the gate to be unlocked, etc., etc. So instead of going through another fuss, Laureen told Sonny to proceed to his place in Sayville. She was anxious to meet his friend. They could retrieve the car some other time.

The house was a refurbished oldie, a bluish-gray clapboard with red door, white porch, and bay window at the side corner. In the living room, Sonny'd collected an odd arrangement of furnishings: an Eastlake rocker with, as he bragged, its original black horsehair upholstery (which nobody ever sat in, he added); a sexily-fringed Récamier in gold silk (only for lounging) and a certified Empire lamp (totally Jacques-Louis David). There, too, were comfortably modern cream-colored leather furnishings, a couch and an armchair, at right angle to each other; two chrome-and-black-leather Eames chairs; and on the Persian-melon-colored walls hung, he pointed out, a zany, yellowy Chagall and a vector-driven Kandinsky (both probable fakes; otherwise, he'd have been crazy not to insure them for millions).

"But who would know the difference, hah?" The answer was no one, except maybe the assessors on the Channel 13 *Antiques Road Show*; an act he intended to join in the very distant future.

"There's always Sotheby's," suggested Laureen.

"Forget that," said Sonny. He took her coat and hung it in the entranceway.

Within ten minutes the guest arrived. He was introduced as Neville Davis, Dean of Instruction at Peconic College: a tall, dark, handsome African American, perfectly dressed in plaid button-down-collar sport shirt, neat trousers, and tan brushed-leather deck shoes. Sonny took his maroon leather coat and tossed it on the staircase leading upstairs. Quietly, he handed Sonny a plastic supermarket bag, within which Laureen saw something heavy wrapped in newspaper. Sonny took the bag and brought it into another room, then stuck his head back into the living room to say:

"It's okay. You two can start talking."

She and Neville both laughed.

"Let's sit," the fellow offered. She sat in the cream-colored leather armchair, he at the far end of the couch. "How long have you known Sonny?" he asked.

"Since last night," she said. "About ten years before that, on and off for two or three years."

"Then you don't know him that well," he suggested.

"Well enough," she replied, with one raised eyebrow and an intonation that made him laugh quietly.

A cautious man, she said to herself: best to keep things light.

"You're Rodger Metcalf's wife," he practically whispered.

She nodded. He nodded.

"He knew Tom Flynn."

"Quite well."

"So I understand. So I understand." He was barely audible. A small smile appeared on his lips: "I knew him too."

Laureen caught herself staring wide-eyed at Neville Davis. She smiled back at him. Oddly, she began to consider how Mr. Davis might be her witness, her rock.

"Oh," he continued, breaking the slight pause, "you might know my wife. Rochelle Davis? President of the Suffolk County Council on Racial Matters? A. k. a. the CRM. Not a vocal organization these days, except here in Suffolk County. Thanks to Rochelle."

"Yes," she replied. "I see her picture in the paper from time to time. I interviewed her once, briefly."

"Of course," Neville nodded. "I mean, I know you from your *Newsday* articles. I understand that you're being considered for a Pulitzer Prize." She tilted her head towards him, modestly. "Good luck." He breathed. "So many talented women these days."

"The talent was always there. It just needed the opportunity."

"Precisely."

This was stifling. She saw the door closing on Mr. Davis. She wanted to rise from her armchair, nod to the fellow, shout goodbye to Sonny--who was more of a soft tomato than a rock--and go home. Trouble was, Sonny drove her directly to his house here in Sayville, while her car, that non-descript dark gray Toyota, stayed parked at the college.

Then, again, there was that hint: and she could just sit there and think about the connection between Neville Davis and Tom Flynn and wonder to what purpose she could put a suave, cautious college dean.

In her despair, Laureen revived a slight hope that, apropos of Sonny's promise, this gentle bureaucrat had something for her. Some gift, some enlightenment. Some opening into the mysteries of the day. Sitting here, she felt baffled, anxious. Why hadn't she confronted Van Dam in the police station? But here re-entered Sonny Anzalone in his flowing satin pineapple splendor, holding two cocktail glasses with red and white swirling peppermint-stick stems.

"The rule is," he said,, "when the night is dark, Manhattans; when the light is bright, martinis. *Nicht vahr?*" He set the peppermint-stick cocktail glasses down on the white linen strip on the coffee table, a thick ebony piece with curved legs ending in claws.

Both Neville and she stood, as Laureen noticed the day outside was hardly bright. Both protested that the afternoon had barely begun and they needed to get going; but Sonny, ignoring them, went back and forth from the kitchen, filling the coffee table with crackers, herring, sliced egg, mixed nuts, dried apricots, and three wedges of cheese. He jostled them into eating and then drinking; he poured the martinis from a clear glass pitcher and plopped in green olives. Laureen mentioned her excess the night before; but he talked about a hair of the dog, about her being Irish and capable of drinking them both under the coffee table. He was so humorous she gave in. So did Neville.

She resigned herself to losing the day. Admittedly, she wanted to lose the day.

"Isn't this better than sitting home alone, crying your heart out?"

"No," she replied. Still, she sipped.

"So," Sonny began, "this is a coincidence, our meeting like this. Neville, by some crazy chance, happens to know something about your Rodger."

Neville cleared his throat.

"I do." He sipped his drink.

Laureen waited.

"He phoned me last night, explaining that he might have to miss a week of school. He told me that he'd gotten involved in the business of Tom Flynn and his death. I believe he has a law degree. So I suppose it involves a question of the Flynns' estate. He once acted as legal counsel for Tom Flynn. A while ago, that is."

"Where is he now?" she asked.

He smiled, shrugging. She sipped her martini.

So that was it. That was the big news, that her husband might miss a week of school in order to interpret Tom Flynn's will? Rubbish. She thought again: he'd miss a week. That went nowhere. And any connection with Sandra . . . went nowhere. She gazed at the man--a study in caution--to see how he might serve some better purpose.

He was handsome, this Neville Davis, with manners smooth as silk. As she began to feel more relaxed; for the hair of the dog had its effect; she wondered how it would be to have an affair with such a man, tall, very dark, and somewhat sexless. Did he have the trace of a Caribbean accent, she wondered. Interesting. A good transition into single life. Her marriage with the student-seducing Rodger was over; they'd had, all along, their fights about his fucking pheromones. There'd been a lull, but now this last jaunt of his . . . no good. Then, too, he might have already left her. All part of life's little ironies.

As Neville and Sonny got to talking about something between them, Laureen thought back upon these past summer days when she spent all her time in county offices, reading papers and interviewing minor bureaucrats. It had been more than two weeks since the last of her articles appeared. Since then, she felt as if she'd entered a void and then a whirlpool. She'd never played around while married to Rodger, sex not being the most important thing to her. But a short liaison with an intelligent, pleasant-smiling fellow like Neville--what the hell. So what if he was mostly interested in men. So what if he was married. When you got down to it, life was a frivolous thing. Anyway, it was time for a break. He was married, and that would provide her with an excuse to end the affair early. He, a college dean, would make a perfect witness, wouldn't he? Yes, but not if he and she were having a little you-know-what together. While she mused on other possibilities, other men in her work-world, she shook her head to clear it of nonsense. That's when her attention suddenly brought her back to the quiet party as she heard

Sonny whisper the word "pistol" and then saw him covering his mouth with his hand and rolling his eyes upward.

"Pistol?" she echoed.

The two men looked at each other. Sonny giggled; Neville looked somber.

"I know what it's like to shoot a pistol," she stated.

"I wouldn't," Sonny said quickly.

Neville shook his head: he wouldn't, either.

"Fun," she went on, surprised at her own humor, "as long as you're not killing anyone."

The two men looked at each other, then back at Laureen. Neville took a deep breath and said:

"Sonny, bring me that bag I handed you as I came in."

Sonny glanced at him, eyebrow raised, as if to say, in mock seriousness, "Are you sure?"

Neville nodded.

"If that would ease the tension," Sonny rose and fetched Neville's package: the plastic bag with a heavy thing wrapped in newspaper: a pistol, a black Smith & Wesson, the kind used by the police.

"This is the main reason I agreed to meet you today," Neville began. "I believe you and Sandra Flynn were close at one time." He looked for a reaction, but Laureen remained silent. "I believe you had some emotional interest in the death of her husband." She nodded. "You might have thought," he continued, "that your news articles had something to do with his suicide. Now, with Sandra's death, well, Sonny mentioned to me that you were not quite yourself last night." He smiled a soft, understanding smile. Briefly, he glanced aside with wistful, melancholy eyes. "I understand that yesterday was unusually stressful, Laureen; I mean, if you'll excuse my saying so, that things are not good between you and your husband." He paused. She said nothing. "Perhaps I'm moving too fast."

She shook her head.

"Then I'll get to the point. I tried to ease your mind about your husband just now. What I know about Rodger Metcalf and the police may have no substance. On the other hand, correct me if I'm wrong: I believe you suspect that Rodger might have been arrested in either Tom or Sandra's death."

Sandra's, yes. But now Tom's? Tom's?

"Tom may have committed suicide," Neville commented, "but maybe not: this may have been the pistol that killed him." He brandished it, holding it in the middle, with the trigger guard in his palm and the barrel to the ceiling. He twisted it one way, then another.

Laureen wanted to say that she'd been to the county morgue and been told that the pistol believed to have been used in the killing was a .22; but she restrained herself, thinking it better to hear Neville to the end.

"It's my gun," he averred, "though I've never used it."

"Do you have a license for it?" asked Sonny.

"No," replied Neville, staring hard at Sonny. "I got it through a friend."

"Oh," said Sonny, leaning and pouring everyone a second martini. "It's not that hard to get, a gun license. You just ask for a form at the police station and fill it out."

"If you're white," corrected Neville.

"We can't all be white," Sonny said with a shrug, sipping his drink.

"Precisely." Neville turned to Laureen. "A few years ago there was a string of robberies in my neighborhood; I live in Dix Hills; and some residents there reported a prowler. So I thought it wise to be prepared." He placed the pistol on the white linen cloth on the ebony coffee table and glanced back at Laureen.

Sitting forward, she pushed her short black hair back on one side several times. "Then if you've never used it . . . ."

"My wife," Neville said simply. "She might have."

She reacted with a wide-eyed stare. Then as she tilted her head back to one side, her eyes could not have squinted more shrewdly. His wife, Rochelle Davis, President of the CRM in Suffolk County, the murderer of Tom Flynn?

"Sounds crazy, I know," admitted the college's Dean of Instruction, as Laureen remembered his position, smiling to herself. "But listen. I found this thing in a place I did not put it. Okay? I keep it in a boot, a cowboy boot, which along with its partner I never wear: of alligator hide, bought one year in Mexico. But where did I find it? On the other side of my walk-in closet in a pair of ski boots which I generally use several times during the winter. I was checking them, just going over my ski equipment, when the gun fell out."

"Jesus," said Sonny. "That could've happened to anyone."

"Listen," countered Neville, with a stern look at Sonny, holding the ess-sound. "Normally, I would've wondered about the oddity of that and then in another hour forgotten it. But then I remembered Rochelle, my wife, and her ranting, on and on through the election campaign, how she

was not too happy with you"--he nodded toward Laureen--
"but how she absolutely hated Tom Flynn!"

"I never saw much in him myself," commented Sonny.

"Shut up," said his friend.

Sonny, continuing to sip, held up an open palm and
waved it daintily at him.

"She wondered how much it would cost to have him
killed."

"Really," said Laureen.

"Really. Now, as they say in the courtroom, this is all
conjecture. But her attitude, you might call it, was queer.
She could hardly sit still during the last month, hardly stay
in the house. And the ranting never stopped. Of course,
they were losing the election big time. I say they, meaning
the gentlemen she consorted with, one gentleman in
particular, Frank Van Dam."

"I understand," said Laureen, "that she would've been
under a lot of stress, with her cohorts losing and all--but . . .
why . . .?" She felt her cheeks getting hot.

"Money? Surely, you of all people might see that. There
was a question, as you so deftly revealed it in your exposé,
of seventeen million dollars."

"Okay."

"They didn't know where it was."

"They?"

"She and Van Dam."

"Oh."

"Flynn did."

"Oh."

"They all did at one time. But then Van Dam outsmarted
himself by having Flynn move it around outside the

country on his own. Flynn was going to make it all right once the scandal blew over. But then he got panicky when your articles named him, and he thought he might go to prison. In short, he intended to leave the country, so they believed, and keep the money for himself in Brazil or some such place."

"Oh," she said, and then: "Yes." As if by inspiration, she placed her half-finished martini on the coffee table and vowed to stop drinking forever. While the truth of Neville's allegations remained open to doubt, their ambiguity had the effect of reviving in her that channel of lively thought, the need for further investigation. That introduction of Rochelle Davis into the case struck Laureen like a touch of morning light. Rochelle and Van Dam! And then, those two and Sandra! A weird connection, if not simply a blind alley. Her next utterance was: "Why?" Why, that is, would Neville speak his mind so frankly, especially in view of Rochelle's being his wife?

He claimed that he wanted to protect his wife from any investigation. He was, after all, proceeding on conjecture. Perhaps he was wrong. He wanted to be wrong. Therefore, he wanted Laureen to take his gun and see if she could have someone determine if it had been fired recently. It seemed clean to him, but what did he know? An analysis would reveal everything. However, he couldn't very well go around looking for a lab test, since what would anyone suppose of a dark-skinned man with a pistol, a black Smith & Wesson? If it had been fired recently, he was sure to be arrested. He couldn't have Sonny do the legwork, either, for obvious reasons, he added with a slight smile. In fact, it was Sonny who'd begged off and at the same time suggested her, because people took her seriously and understood that her work as a reporter was a plausible reason for her interest in curious firearms.

I'm black too, thought Laureen. Some men these were. Then, "Fine," she said, "I'll take it." She breathed slowly and deeply. Studying Neville's face as he spoke, she had the suspicion that he could indeed be of service to her. There was a steadiness to the man, for all his strangeness. And because of all his strangeness, he might be approachable where other men weren't. Certainly, he was a better bet than Sonny. She leaned forward and picked up the gun with a napkin. Holding it barrel down in Sonny's direction, she ordered him to wrap it up.

"Now," added Neville, "as I thank you, I must also warn you that if anything incriminating arises in the course of your research, I will deny I or my wife ever saw that thing."

"So will I," said Sonny, "and I don't even have a wife."

"Fine," she responded, understanding that any fingerprints had been wiped off, while giving the vague impression that she would know how to dispose of the piece in safety. She couldn't say what she would do if she discovered that the gun had been fired recently. If there was none of the woman's fingerprints on the gun, that would kill the case from the start. This pistol could lead nowhere. Though, possibly, it might have some connection with Van Dam? Something Rochelle might confess to? Something tangible?

"I knew Tom Flynn quite well," Neville had begun to speak again, "once. I would hate to suppose that my wife or anyone else had a hand in his death." He rose to leave, nodding his thanks to Sonny, who also rose.

"I hope you mean to say something nice about me before you go, Neville. I refer to your insinuation that I couldn't possibly handle anything so serious as a pistol. Who do you think would've done the job if Laureen here didn't accept?"

The man had to stare at him for a few seconds to determine whether he was joking or not. "Oh, stuff it," he finally said.

"*Prosit.*" Sonny lifted his cocktail glass to his friend, then sipped.

"*Prosit* yourself, Sonny," responded Neville, whose bland, handsome faced altered into a hard, mean expression. "Don't think," he said, "that I came here looking for your support or affection. Or whatever consolation you'd have to offer me." His dark eyes were riveted on Sonny's. "If I'd ever found a momentary pleasure or bit of fun, as you might phrase it, it ended a long time ago. It had no substance, see. My nature, my real nature, doesn't tend in that direction. So, please, let's not dwell on things that never happened."

Laureen listened with mild shock. The man was insisting, it seemed, that he wasn't, well, gay.

Collecting himself, he apologized for the outburst, explaining that lately he'd been under a lot of stress. He gave her a business card and asked her to contact him at her convenience. Shaking her hand, he thanked her several times, nodding his head in affirmation.

"I hope to see you again," said Laureen, as he walked to the door and left.

"Ain't that a kick in the head," commented Sonny, who sat and poured himself another martini.

When she inquired into the *prosit* routine, Sonny spoke sarcastically out of the side of his mouth, telling her that Neville and he had vacationed one summer in Berlin a long, long time ago. They'd gotten into the habit of toasting each other in German. It all ended when they returned to the States, where they remained friendly off and on.

"He's always afraid I'm going to come on to him again," he said. "You know, start groping him in public."

"But his wife?"

"Oh, I'm sure he loves her in his own peculiar way."

"And Tom Flynn?"

"Torrid, torrid," Sonny emphasized the word. "Not a long, long time ago, just some years back, about ten or so. Remember that big bird controversy out in the Hamptons, back in the Nineties? Remember that sculptor Stanko?"

"Sure," she said, "I interviewed him. His big bird was a thirty-foot-high pink flamingo." It was simply amazing how . . . . But she didn't finish the thought.

"Yes. Well, Stanko was my best friend at the time. I can't tell why now, but maybe it had something to do with my fixation on flamingos. Ever since, yes, well, I've told you that story already. Anyway, during the hullaballoo over the big pink bird, Neville attended a debate in Hampton Bays. He came over to Stanko's house afterwards to a symposium or, as the Greeks would have it, a drinking orgy. There he met the Saviors of County Liberty, the Brutus and Cassius of the Local Party, those young troublemakers, Tom Flynn and Rodger Metcalf.

Your husband left immediately on seeing the kind of crowd it was; but Mr. Flynn stayed on. That's when Neville discovered that this eager politician was eager in other ways. And so it went for several months. Then it didn't. Neville was married. His wife was political. Our Mr. Flynn, his heart as conventional as Neville's, also believed himself to be the marrying kind. The rest you know. He married your lovely friend Sandra."

He helped Laureen on with her coat, then handed her the bag with the gun.

"Just a little bundle," he said. "Others' lives are so much more burdensome." When he saw the squint in her eyes, he covered his tracks with: "Consider this, at least: If Tom was killed by someone, you know now that it probably wasn't Sandra."

But possibly Rochelle Davis. And did she bludgeon Sandra Flynn, as well? No, that was Van Dam, Van Dam, Van Dam. But if Tom Flynn was murdered, that left the question of a connection to the murder of Sandra Flynn.

When she paused in the entranceway, he gave her an inquiring look.

"Have you forgotten?" she asked. "You need to drive me back to the school."

Sonny slapped his forehead.

"Why do you drive a Mini Cooper?" she wondered once they were on their way.

"The police never stop a Mini Cooper," he explained gaily. "It's insignificant, virtually invisible. In this little thing I can drive drunk all I want."

Neither spoke during the next fifteen minutes.

Then out of nowhere Sonny said, "And about Sandra and me. I made it all up. It never happened."

Laureen did not respond. It could hardly matter whether he was lying or not. She speculated, instead, on Sonny's dopey remark about burdens. It had some truth to it. Other people seemed to have problems much more complex than one's own. They thrashed about in life, tragically, comically. Ruefully, she contemplated how everything and everybody seemed to be connected; and, further, how everyone stumbled about in his own deep delusions, including herself.

Beneath all this speculation, she felt the need to hold onto Neville Davis. Some rock. She wondered how she could write anything solid about Sandra with all of these new bits and pieces flying around in the air. She wondered how she might construct a scene with a witness that would convict Frank Van Dam.

CHAPTER NINE
Ships That Pass in the Night

Laureen pursued the connection between Van Dam and Rochelle Davis, wondering why the woman's husband would've brought her into suspicion in what was agreed to be a case of suicide. To be arrested for gun possession in New York State is not desirable; yet Neville might've disposed of the piece by tossing it into the Long Island Sound. True, he needed to be sure of his wife's non-involvement with Flynn's death. Could anyone be sure that those damning words were actually hers? Was Neville stable? His verbal attack on Sonny was pretty nasty-- uncalled-for in front of her. Further on, and aside from the outburst, Laureen would help with the pistol, still wondering if there was something psychic in his intention, an irrational need to contact her through Sonny. To tell her what?

She slept late again. When the mail came at eleven, it brought the envelope with the papers Sandra promised her. In the kitchen she removed the material, read it quickly, with its numerous references to Van Dam, all damning; damning, too, to Rochelle Davis. Even better, the writing was Flynn's, and that could be proven; so the document would hold up in court. And the money? Hidden away in three countries, Brazil, Switzerland, and the Bahamas.

She slid the papers under her living room carpet. Then she drove to Morgan's Gun Shop in Hauppauge, where her police cadet instructor, Bill Evashevski, was manager. They'd remained friends after she decided to leave the academy; she'd gotten interested, though, in pistol range practice, and Bill would meet her at the range and help polish her style. She did an article on him once, as a retired cop who kept active in the field of firearms; and he helped answer her questions on topics she wrote about, such as rabid raccoon hunting in Suffolk County and gang gun-favorites in the dangerous neighborhoods. It took him less than two minutes to determine that Neville's pistol had been fired.

"It's a common firearm used by U. S. Army MPs a decade ago," he told her, brandishing it with plastic gloves on his hands, "and that's all I can tell you, because, between you and me, I never saw it." He dropped the thing into her plastic bag. "I never saw you, either. Now, get out of here."

She arranged to meet Neville later that day, and at five-thirty he welcomed her into his handsome colonial. The foyer had a slate floor and a staircase curving up to the next landing. The furnishings were typically upper middle-class: nice, but undistinguished, even in color, which was a mix of brown woods and pale colors on walls and upholstery. In his socks, the man, suave as ever, wore a white Oxford button-down shirt and velvety blue corduroy trousers. He brought her into the living room, had her sit on the long pale-orange couch, and asked her what she'd like to drink.

"Big trouble," she said, raising an eyebrow and placing the pistol, still in its wrapping, on the coffee table.

He glanced down at it.

With a fallen face he nodded and sat in the armchair adjacent to Laureen. He leaned toward her, resting his elbows on his knees, clasping his hands. "It's been used?" he needed confirmation.

"Yes," she said.

"Really."

"Not good," she stated.

"Guess not."

"And that leaves me with a few questions," she went on.

"Oh?" He leaned back, his hands on the armrests.

"Number one: how do I know you didn't use it to kill Flynn?" she said.

He smiled weakly. "If I did, why would I seek you out?"

"To cover your tracks?"

"Really, now."

"Okay. Number two: do I get to meet your wife?" she looked one way and another. Wasn't the woman at home?

"Some day, I guess," replied Neville. "Is that what you expected in coming here?"

Laureen shrugged.

"I thought I'd mentioned something at Sonny's place. My wife is in Albany," he said, suppressing an angry tightening in his neck. He breathed deeply.

"Oh, I see."

"She goes there with other politicians at least once a month. Frank Van Dam goes there also." He paused. "She's due to be home tomorrow."

His quiet hysteria fascinated her, particularly for its allusion to Van Dam. She had no regrets in not seeing the man's wife. She almost giggled when she thought of Rochelle Davis in a lurid liaison with the red-haired Party Leader--black and white, murderer and murderess. Could she use Mr. Davis and his jealousy to get Van Dam?

"Okay," she said, trying to keep focused, "why bring your wife into this mess? If you were so anxious to protect her, you might've kept quiet and left well enough alone."

"That's true," he said, looking briefly at the ceiling, then back at Laureen. "You could say I panicked. Sometimes we bring on the worst by overreacting."

She waited, hearing his breathing.

"I came here to listen," she said, thinking: he came to me with the Smith & Wesson; perhaps he'll come to me with a plan--at least, the suggestion of one. He'd love to get Van Dam out of the picture.

He, however, went into his own, one might say, peculiarity.

"I have these, how shall I call them, insights. Rarely, of course, not every day; not even every year. My mother, you know, came from the Islands; she believed in a lot of nonsense, you see, and I grew up believing in a lot of it myself: about charms and such, about dreams and ghosts. You understand. Once I'd been through college, I put all that aside. Yet I'd have dreams that came true, premonitions of disaster. My father died in a car accident that I pictured in my mind on that very day as I sat in my office in the college, thinking of nothing. Consider my reaction. It was terrible: terrible to witness and terrible to live with." He swallowed. "How about a glass of mineral water?" he offered.

"Fine," she said.

Returning from the kitchen, he set the glasses down on coasters on the coffee table.

"Now you might guess what I have to tell you."

Laureen shook her head.

"I saw Tom Flynn, hunched over his desk, blood oozing from his head." He sighed. "We'd known each other briefly. I'd thought about him from time to time. And then there he was. I saw him in my mind's eye. It was early in the morning as I lay in bed. I hadn't slept all night." He paused to watch her reaction. "Later that day there it was, on the news. When I came home, I went to my clothes closet to check on that pistol. It wasn't where I'd put it. So I got scared."

She said nothing.

"In my vision," he continued, "I saw dollar signs. I saw the man's tie. It was yellow and blue."

She nodded. "And the gun?"

"No I didn't see it. Oh, you mean the Smith & Wesson, while the lab claimed it to be a .22?" Neville smiled. "Labs make mistakes."

"But you wanted to prove your wife innocent," pursued Laureen. "I mean, how did you suppose it got removed from your cowboy boot and put in your ski boot?"

"I could only imagine," he answered, "that my wife had found it . . . maybe carried it around for a while . . . then put it back in the wrong spot. Obviously, I needed to confirm her innocence." His weak smile seemed framed in a face about to cry.

Interesting woman, thought Laureen, if that was all she did with the gun, carry it around for a few days: except if it hadn't been fired that once. By her or Mr. Van Dam.

As for Neville, he still hadn't given her a straight answer about Tom. There'd been no mention of the tie in any news report. How could he have known about the tie or those dollars signs, she wondered, unless he'd been in the office where Flynn died?

"You . . . ?" she didn't finish, just raised her eyebrow.

Staring at her for a long time, he answered by simply moving his head back and forth very slowly.

"Sorry," she said. "I had to . . . ." Stay focused, she told herself. This dude might be a paranoid schizophrenic who shot Tom Flynn while only dreaming he had.

"There was no bitterness," he continued, "after we . . . . ."

"I understand," she nodded, smiling a bit.

"I suppose what started me thinking about him was Rochelle and all her disgusting comments. He'd been in the newspaper for the past several weeks."

Laureen turned her smile into a soft grimace.

"Perhaps you'd like to understand something about Rochelle and me." His sipped his water. "I'm not a homosexual, in spite of what Sonny might say. True, I've taken excursions, but perhaps you can relate . . . well, I apologize: I'll leave that alone. I, uh, I love my wife, Laureen. It's just that . . . ." His voice had gotten strangely high-pitched. He didn't finish. He swallowed and changed the subject. He took a drink from his glass of water. He needed to explain himself. Here followed an account of the domestic scene late Friday as Rochelle prepared to leave for Albany.

They'd argued about her spending the weekend upstate: strictly on business, as she claimed; but, as he claimed, in an arrangement with Mr. Van Dam.

"An affair?" Laureen ventured. This was the link she sought. The suavely white Frank Van Dam and the visibly black leader of the Suffolk County CRM. Was that not ironic? But, shut up, she told herself; concentrate.

"I've never been sure," Neville explained. "I'd thought I'd push her a bit, you know, get her to admit an affection for him, for Mr. Van Dam. They work hand-in-glove on county politics. She helped draft that low-income housing measure that became fairly successful. And then they ate together a few times a month, with all the other politicians who feed at the county trough."

Frequently, Rochelle and he argued about each other's loyalty, she claiming, in view of his accusation about her and Van Dam, that he'd gone into a deep depression over the death of Tom Flynn. Not true. In fact, as they fought, he became aroused by her as she strutted around the bedroom, choosing clothes to wear for her trip. No one could be sexier than Rochelle in provocative lingerie. "Pink lingerie," he added. "It's always made me weak, right in here." He touched his solar plexus. "Especially with lace."

He needed to explain further. Right then, as his wife slipped into a tight black leather skirt, another incitement to arousal, he'd knelt before her on an erotic impulse and kissed her feet. Then he moved up her legs, finally burying his head in her stomach, bulging slightly under the leather, as he solicited her memory of the days before their marriage. He desired her at that moment with the same "passion" (he spoke the word as if in quotation marks) as that time in the woods in New Jersey, near a lake, when they were alone and it was springtime. And so, on Friday evening, as once in New Jersey by a lake, she removed her skirt, and they made love. He was "passionate"; while she, however, had risen from the bed and continued to pack for the weekend.

He spoke with emotion. Laureen didn't need to hear all the lovely nuances of this escapade with his own wife. It seemed voyeuristic and, for him, much in the way of overcompensation.

"I've always been astonished to consider," he said pathetically, "how much she and I have in common--background, education, tastes--and how little we ever agree on anything."

He continued. " 'Do you know what we are?' she said to me as she prepared to leave. 'Two ships that pass in the night.' Clichéd but true."

It was time to move the agenda.

"Let's talk about Tom Flynn and Frank Van Dam," Laureen suggested. "You mentioned at Sonny's place that your wife believed that Mr. Flynn had a great deal of money hidden somewhere outside the country. In a location known only to him."

"Well, yes." He was more reluctant on this topic.

"Mr. Davis, Neville," she said, "I'm a reporter for a large newspaper. What can I tell you, I mean how can I assure you that this, more than anything, is a personal matter for me? But there is something I couldn't tell you yesterday." She looked him in the eye. "I know where that money is. Don't ask how. I always protect my sources."

"Really."

"Both Frank Van Dam and your wife, well, they are implicated in the theft."

He looked at the floor.

"But I don't think they know where the money is."

"I found out only this morning," said Laureen.

"Then why haven't you gone to the police?" he asked.

"Frankly, I'm not sure how to proceed."

"How deeply is Rochelle . . . ?" he couldn't finish.

He shook his head, waved his hand. He needed to change the subject.

He stood and paced about the living room, hands in his blue corduroy trouser pockets. He kept shaking his head. It seemed he wanted to gesture as he spoke; the pockets were there to keep his arms and hands from extravagance. His dark face, however, became animated. Could he deal with the issue of his wife's being brought to trial? Not yet. Instead, he wondered why in the throes of the scandal about the seventeen million dollars nobody--and that nobody including the newswoman who wrote about it--ever went after Frank Van Dam. At least he was back to the main issue

"If you know so much about it," he asked, "why doesn't anyone else?"

"The perpetrators know."

"We'll have to discuss the full implications at another time. But as for Tom and his wife, I have some interesting thoughts. He may have committed suicide; she may have been bludgeoned to death by an intruder looking for money. That may be all there is to these cases. On the other hand . . . I think," Neville said slowly, still looking at the floor, "that the two deaths are related."

She was puzzled. He was moving in another direction.

"I had a dream last night," he explained, staring straight ahead. "Last night as I lay sleeping alone in my bed, I saw a man and a woman stretched out on the beach. Naked.

An old white-haired man stood chest-high in the onrushing waves that churned up sea-foam all around the couple, and then as the water receded it carried the bodies of the man and woman back out towards the white-haired fellow, who, as if he were blind, stood still, making no move to save them, letting them pass by as the current bore them into the ocean."

He paused.

"I woke in a cold sweat," he continued. "I knew I'd been dreaming of death."

"Fascinating."

"That's all I know."

"Really . . . interesting," she said. "But let's go back again to my question about Tom and the two politicians, your wife and Frank."

He didn't get it. He had no idea of tackling the Boy Wonder, no matter what the man was doing with his wife. No matter what the justice of the case was. Nothing practical, just dreams. She'd overstepped herself, clumsily. She should've gone more slowly. Still, she needed to explain . . . something.

"I don't think Flynn's death involves your wife, not directly—though there is the money-question. From what I understand, the forensics lab has already established that a .22 Luger killed Flynn. True, they make mistakes; but . . . ." She tried to look into his eyes, but he looked up and off to the side, as if he heard her voice from another part of the house. "For her part, maybe Rochelle took the Smith & Wesson to a firing range for fun or something. Or gave it to Frank Van Dam. We might be able to establish a connection--with one or two murderers, perhaps--even in the form of a threat. In a word that Van Dam spoke to her. Something that made her offer the gun to him. Honestly, Neville, I thought you might help." She handed him her business card. She looked hard into his dark eyes as he finally peered down at hers.

"I will," he agreed, studying the card. "But . . . ."

"And I'll keep the gun," she said, "for now."

He nodded.

"As for Rochelle and the money . . ." she wanted to add that some kind of deal might be available if she could help in the prosecution of Van Dam.

"But don't you see the meaning of my dream?" he asked, impatiently.

She bit the side of her upper lip, shaking her head.

"Their deaths are linked. Sandra's killer was also in some way Tom's." He stood still, nodding his head in certainty. "It's disturbing to think that my wife not only . . . ." He didn't finish.

"Who was the white-haired guy in the water?" she asked.

"I can't say for sure. But . . . but I've seen him before," he said hesitantly, "and I have my suspicions."

Seen him before, well. It was as if Neville had some kind of ongoing intercourse with phantoms--as, in her dream, so did she. She raised her eyebrows. It was as if she needed to find this guy, if he could be any help at all, somewhere in psychic space.

"I thought I saw him on the beach in Westhampton after that giant flamingo collapsed. Actually, I thought I saw him in the water, chest high, just as in my dream." He gazed at Laureen, awaiting her response; but she remained silent. "And then not long after that I thought I saw him on the side of the road as I drove one night on Southern State Parkway. Do you remember Arthur Weisskoff, the politician who--"

"Yes," she cut him off, "of course I remember." That was enough. She stood. She felt strange, detached. The house was warm, overheated. She needed to leave. She didn't approve of giving in to panic, but that drowning feeling came over her. It was as if the two of them, she and Neville, had ascended into another sphere of consciousness. Neville, for his part, recognized her discomfort and, without being asked, got her overcoat and helped her on with it.

"Would you," she forced herself to speak, as she turned from the door, "would you consider a plan"--god, was this difficult--"I mean, a way, to get Van Dam to reveal himself . . . as a murderer?"

His eyes widened. He'd swallowed hard and licked his lips. His face showed no expression. "If it would save Rochelle."

She'd frightened him. Some rock.

On her way home Laureen, depressed and desperate over Neville's failure as a rock, tried to see a logical development out of the man's potpourri of dreams, conjectures, and insinuations. She'd hoped to find a link between Tom Flynn's peculations and the inner workings of the party led by Frank Van Dam, perhaps by elaborating on Rochelle Davis' liaison with the Boy Wonder. As for Rodger, there was no way in the world he could be implicated beyond the business, over ten years ago, of draining a gas line as a prank. Even more puzzling was the dream of the two bodies. Begrudgingly, she acknowledged that Neville had drawn her into his field of psychic vision--suggestively putting the two Flynns together in death. Perhaps that was all that it meant, simply that they'd died within days of each other. The image of Arthur Weisskoff, if that's who it was, symbolized, perhaps, the passage to the world beyond, since that was where he himself had passed. And then the color of Flynn's tie. Was that a flash of ESP, merely that and nothing more? "Merely that and nothing more." That was a line from . . . from . . . from--and trying to remember her high school days and the poems she'd read in English class, she felt her nose begin to run again. That's when she bumped into the car in front of her as the title "The Raven" popped into her head.

Rather, her head popped against the windshield, and she passed into brief unconsciousness.

Her own fault. She should have kept her eyes on the road. She recalled later that traffic had slowed down in a rush-hour crawl on the Long Island Expressway. She'd slowed too, but then she'd misjudged the speed of the other cars, and that was when it happened: Bump!

She'd been unconscious only some few seconds at most and partially aware of what happened. She came to as a man shouted at her through the door window: "Are you all right?"

"Yes, yes," she whispered.

She opened the car door and stood out on the highway. The man, suppressing his frustration, requested her driver's license and insurance card. He helped her write down his own information. She refused his offer to phone for an ambulance. She didn't want to go to a hospital, suspecting she might be kept there for a few days. She worried about the nurses finding the pistol in her purse. The man shrugged. It was her life. Rubberneckers slowed their vehicles to peer into her business; and sped off, as traffic had, ironically, lightened and moved along with perfunctory briskness.

If she'd only stayed five minutes longer at the Davis' place, this wouldn't have happened. How disappointing he was. She sighed, driving away and wondering at the absurdity of cause and effect in the real world. She couldn't wonder, however, with any philosophical complexity because, as she suspected, she'd gotten a concussion and had already begun to forget the outline of the accident.

Laureen tried to overcome the sleepiness that made her head heavy, her thoughts murky. At home she made strong coffee, drank three cups, and walked around the house, upstairs and down. At eight o'clock, she went and lay in bed. As a haziness gathered around her, she heard the front doorknob rattling, then several gentle knocks. When the knocks got louder, she sat up, her heart beating, her breath short. With appalling suddenness she thought of the pistol she had in her purse; and with the swiftness of hysteria, she saw the possibility that someone--Rodger or Frank or Rochelle--might have one also and had decided to come and kill her! Certainly, Rochelle. By now her husband had told her everything. She'd have believed that Laureen was alone, that her husband had deserted her, and that she could easily force her way into her house. Perhaps she'd bludgeon her to death as she had killed Sandra. But, no, the woman was a hundred and fifty miles away in Albany.

Then maybe it was Frank Van Dam! Wildly she tried to conceive how she could use the pistol without bullets in it!

Sandra, she reminded herself, had been hit with a blunt object. Serial killers, she knew, did not vary in their death-techniques. Tom had been shot with a pistol. Shaking her head and calming herself, she rose and got the black gun from her purse. She stood still, in a near-trance, feeling as if she were in a play. The script was written and she had to act to save herself. Bravely, she left her bedroom and came to the window in her living room. She held the gun pressed against her chest.

"Laureen! Laureen!" shouted the knocker, immediately identifying himself as her husband. "I know you're home. Open the door!"

Flicking on the porch light, she admitted Rodger. He was haggard; he'd lost his house key; and he needed clothing since he had to work the next day. No, he was not going to take the week off as he'd told Neville Davis. And, no, he wasn't prepared to stay. He'd taken a room at a motel in Bohemia. And, no, he didn't want to talk. When Laureen tried to introduce the subject of Takeesha Montaigne, he waved her off with a weary look on his unshaven face. Briefly, he explained that his reasons were more serious than that; he would have his lawyer contact her and clarify his case.

"Besides," he said, "you never gave me a son."

Or a daughter. That came out of nowhere, paranoid; with no way to answer it.

"Did you kill Sandra?" she demanded.

Rodger paused and stared at her. That's when he saw the gun in her hand, she realized later, pressed against her chest. His jaw dropped. Then he turned and hurriedly collected shirts, slacks, shoes, socks, and underwear, stuffing them into his suitcase and bidding her goodbye. Just that rush and that stupid insult, and one unanswered question. She wished her head weren't so cloudy.

"I'm talking to the D. A.," was all he said.

"And I've got a concussion," she wanted to say. But his ill-tempered hurriedness deserved no comment. Then an idea occurred to her: if she could get him to stay and sleep in his own bed, she would have an opportunity to smother him under a pillow while he slept. Afterwards she could stash him in the freezer in the garage, then dispose of him when she had more time. A good idea, but she'd have to work on it. And then: "Nuts, I'm going nuts."

She watched quietly as he left the house, put the suitcase in his car trunk, and then backed down the driveway. Then she saw that she'd been holding the pistol stiffly against her chest and that he had seen it.

She wanted to laugh but couldn't. She went to the bedroom and lay down again but didn't fall asleep until three or four in the morning, still holding the gun.

CHAPTER TEN
Motel Flamingo

When she awoke at one o'clock in the afternoon, a haunting chill pervaded the house. After showering, she dressed, shivering in the cold bedroom as she slipped into a pair of jeans and a hairy turquoise sweater. She wondered why the house could be so cold. After blowing her runny nose, she forgot about the chill and started fixing her hair, still trying to think. Checking the clock, she couldn't believe the time; and then she was hungry. Cloudily, she thought of making herself a three-egg omelet with cheese, green pepper, and bacon; she thought of fresh cups of coffee, toast, and grape jelly. She remembered her concussion and, leaning forward to check her pupils in the mirror, saw that one of them was wider than the other. She promised herself that after breakfast she would telephone Dr. Buskin and arrange for an appointment. Then she planned to stay in bed and keep warm under the blankets.

She stood still, trying to settle matters. Her frustration over her husband's appearance and disappearance got nowhere. She shrugged. Let him do what he wanted, was her careless sentiment. Let him get convicted of murdering anybody; she didn't care. Let him die. She had no reason to protect him.

She heard a rustling down the hallway, then the click of her front door lock.

"Rodger?" she called out. She waited, then called again.

No answer.

"Is someone in the house?" she yelled and listened for more noises. "Please answer," she said. Where was that gun?   Apparently she'd tossed it somewhere in the bedroom.

"Hello," a woman's voice called back.

"Just a minute." Laureen took a deep breath and, without the gun, came forward out of the bedroom and down the hall.

There, halfway up the stairwell, stood a dark woman in a brown cashmere coat and matching cloth turban, a woman she recognized but failed to find a name for.

"Who are you?" demanded Laureen.

"Excuse me," replied the woman; "but your front door was wide open. I rang the bell several times. I waited. I supposed you wouldn't mind."

"Who are you?"

"Don't you remember me? I'm Rochelle Davis."

"Oh.   Sure.   Rochelle Davis."   Amazing that she'd forgotten the woman's name.   "What are you doing here? What can I do for you?"

Rochelle gave her a puzzled look, then said, "Obviously we need to talk."   The woman lifted a hand to indicate the living room to her right.

"Of course.   I'm sorry.   Please, come up and sit down." She gestured to the couch. Man, oh, man, was she out of it! She made the effort to collect her thoughts, remembering that she'd told Neville Davis that she had evidence of . . . of . . . and here she remembered the briefcase papers she'd slid under the carpet, the very carpet she stood upon. Good God, maybe the woman was here to kill her, just as she'd supposed.   Too late to stop her now.   Perhaps being sociable would be enough. She stopped staring at Rochelle Davis and actually rubbed her eyes.

"Your storm door had also swung wide open," Rochelle noted. "You were going to lose all of your heat."

"I think," said Laureen, "that my husband was in such a hurry--." She didn't finish, realizing that frosty air had poured into the house for hours and hours. Even worse, anyone might've come in at any moment of the night; nobody did: until now; and who was that but none other than Rochelle Davis; who ascended the next three steps up to the main level and stood facing the woman who had visited her husband the day before.

"I don't want to sit," she asserted. She stood on the carpet, right over the papers.

"In that case," Laureen proposed, "why not come into the kitchen? I just woke up, and I need breakfast."

The woman couldn't have had that Smith & Wesson with her now, wherever the devil it might be. Perhaps another one? Rochelle Davis was her enemy, now more than ever. It was she, the possible Pulitzer-Prize-winning reporter, who'd ruined her political party in the recent election. It was she, now, who had the evidence to put her and her boyfriend away for embezzlement of public funds--if not murder. No, she wouldn't just shoot Laureen, who had no money hidden in foreign banks, only a few sheets of paper that at this moment she stood upon.

The possible Pulitzer-Prize-winning reporter didn't have the brains to worry, not today, not with a cold and a concussion that made her head heavy and dim. It was fun somehow to be dim and snot-heavy; so much more relaxing than being responsible: especially with an ace up her sleeve--or under the carpet.

Laureen regretted not waking earlier and shutting the front door. The women might've met somewhere on neutral ground. The visit, however, became slightly amusing when she listened to Rochelle's explanation for walking in.

"I phoned you this morning, and you told me I could come by at one," she said, standing in the kitchen, staring at her.

"I . . . spoke to you . . . this morning?"

"Yes, on the telephone."

"Oh, man."

More strange looks from Rochelle.

"Please," said Laureen, "I really can't remember. Anything. Let me explain. I hit a car in rush hour last evening and got a concussion. As you can hear, I also have a terrible cold. Please sit down. I'm making coffee. Join me."

Jauntily, with a toss of the head, Rochelle overcame her reluctance and sat at the kitchen table. She removed her coat and let it fall back over the kitchen chair, showing a remarkably blue pinstriped business suit and soft pink turtleneck. Meanwhile, Laureen slowly and thoughtfully prepared herself breakfast: coffee and buttered toast for the moment; describing her accident as she tackled the ingredients. At the same time she studied Rochelle: not a difficult task, as the woman was someone whom people noticed the second she entered a room. She was almost as tall as herself. She had brilliant dark eyes, accented with high-arched eyebrows and prominent cheekbones. Her red mouth was wide and sensual; she had a strong neck and jawline. There was nothing delicate about her except her color, a smooth, unvaried cinnamon; in effect, her color was the most beautiful thing about her. It was soft, feminine; it belied the fierceness of the lady tiger beneath-- a quality revealed at once in the woman's voice, direct and self-assured. And this was the woman, the African American woman, with whom Frank Van Dam, the Boy Wonder, carried on an affair?

"All well and good," commented Rochelle as Laureen finished her tale of the Long Island Expressway. "But you had come, hadn't you, from visiting my husband at our house? So I thought I'd return the favor by visiting you at yours. Especially since you have certain information . . . ."

Laureen smiled.

The other continued: "We have money. We'll pay you; we'll pay you very well. I'm not a violent person. But I need to warn you, you're taking chances. I know a lot of people."

"Frank Van Dam, for instance?"

She wondered if Rochelle only worked at giving out that she and Van Dam were lovers--for whatever reason: to drive her husband crazy, get him to leave, who could guess? Or perhaps to get at Laureen, supposing that Van Dam and she were lovers in high school. To get her jealous.

"I spoke to your husband about this. I expected you to show up, sometime. Neville, your husband, is an unusual man," she said, casually.

"They all say that," countered Rochelle, "but I'm an unusual woman." She smiled. "So are you." If smiles could kill. "Perhaps you want him."

Laureen squeezed her lips together to keep from laughing.

"I didn't come to speak of Neville," the other went on. She tipped her head forward with a twist in her smile, adding, "If you want him . . . ." She didn't finish; she merely looked at Laureen from under her eyelids. Then the smile dropped. For a moment neither woman spoke.

"Evidently not," said Laureen.

Rochelle sat erect, drawing her head up tall, an imperious look in her dark eyes. "We're talking about a lot of money, Laureen. We'll buy whatever you have."

"You are intuitive," Laureen stated.

"Then we are both on the same page." The response came in a slight but knowing nod.

"Thing is," said Laureen. "It's somewhere else. I don't keep it here."

"Then where?"

"On the estate. In Belvedere."

"Oh."

"Tom's diary. But I guess you knew that."

No reaction from Rochelle.

"And the deal?"

"Fifty thousand," said Rochelle.

"Can you meet me at the house?" suggested Laureen. "Tomorrow, at eleven?"

Rochelle nodded.

"Good. I'll be there." She waited for the woman to rise, put on her hat and coat, and leave.

But Rochelle remained, staring at her. Then she spoke: "I've heard that your husband has left you. You asked him to." She paused. "Now, I need to tell you about Frank and me. We've made plans. Do you see? I'll be leaving my husband and going with Frank. We spoke this weekend in Albany. We've been a team, and now we'll be a couple. Maybe we'll leave Suffolk County and start up some place else. It doesn't matter where. We've made plans."

"Really," said Laureen in monotone, fixing her eyes on the other's prominent cheekbones and arched eyebrows. The woman was serious. Frank and Rochelle, a couple, a black-and-white couple: wonderful. Her life had gotten so bizarre, she wanted to laugh and howl at once: but Rochelle and Frank--if that didn't take the cake!

"No need to be sarcastic, Mrs. Metcalf," the other answered. "You have a sharp tongue when you write; and in some way I respect that. But you are not writing now, and we are not talking politics."

"What are we talking?" asked the reporter.

"Love; may I call you Laureen?"--Laureen shrugged since the woman had been calling her this right along--"Love, my dear. We are talking about love."

"Then I wish for you what you wish for yourself," said Laureen. Something told her to be optimistic. The woman, instead of threatening, could be useful. Thank you, Neville; and thanks again.

"Do you really?" pursued Rochelle. "You see, I know about you and Frank. I know that you were his first love and that he often thinks of you. He said as much to me. I suspect also that you long to get together with him again. But the both of you have been married. I suspect that that is why you spent so much of your time writing about our party. You aimed to keep Frank thinking about you. You never gave up hope. You know his love is for, well, our kind of people. Now, tell me that I am wrong."

"That is none of your business."

"I wonder. At first, I didn't mind the articles you wrote. They attacked the party, and I hoped they would turn Frank against you. But they only caused him to bring you up more and more in conversation. A woman has a sense of these things. You may call it intuition. My intuition tells me that there is something between you. It tells me that that something has come to a crossroads. Why, now, after the election and after Frank chances to lose his position in the party, did you ask your husband to leave?"

"What goes on between my husband and me is not your concern."

"I believe," Rochelle went on, "that you are suffering from that concussion and perhaps find it difficult to explain yourself, Laureen. But I think I know better."

No reply.

"Was it not so that you might go off with your lost love, as soon as he retrieves all that lost money, and live out your life in paradise?"

Laureen remained more silent than before. She fixed her sight on Rochelle's high cheekbones and arched eyebrows.

"Love is the answer," the woman continued, "or else why didn't you name him in your articles?"

"No evidence."

With a sly smile, Rochelle, having introduced her theme, launched into a description of her weekend in Albany with Frank Van Dam. She intended to confirm the man's devotion to her, needing to dissuade her supposed rival from ever trespassing on her territory. As she spoke of passion, she grew impassioned; so that Laureen, given her satisfaction as well as her surprise, let her go on and on. She was used to listening--and the details here were irresistible.

"Frank Van Dam bowed and kissed my naked feet." So began the Albany tale--or myth--of Frank Van Dam and Rochelle Davis. In spite of her concussion and her runny nose, Laureen remembered all the details later, almost as if, in the shock of hearing the story, she had made them up herself.

There they were, dining with eighty other politicians. They were desperate, Rochelle and Frank, for a place to be alone. So they left the dinner at the hotel where all of them had registered and drove off into the wilds above Albany. After half an hour on dark country roads they found a small motel ("Motel Flamingo"? Laureen wondered, smiling at herself for being silly) with its neon sign blinking into the frosty night. Emerging from the car, they could see the heaviness of their steamy breaths in the chilly night air. He was still slightly drunk when they checked in; still dizzy from the cocktail hour followed by several glasses of red wine at dinner. The motel was seedy, poorly ventilated, with the faint smell of cigarette smoke. The decor was a faded brown: brown walls, brown bedcovers, brown rug. The bathroom fixtures were old. Everything about it spelled cheaters' sleazy sex.

"Third-rate romance, low-rent rendezvous," commented Frank comically. She asked him what he meant, and he told him that he remembered an old song he'd heard on a Country and Western radio station fifteen years ago.

"Third-rate romance, low-rent rendezvous," he repeated laughing.

Impulsively, she slapped his face. "Nothing third-rate about me," she said.

Soberly, he looked at her, then pushed her onto the bed. He was tall; still, his strength surprised her. He surprised her again when he didn't join her there, but rather bent down at the bed's edge and removed her high heels, tossing them off to the side. One of them clattered into the bathroom sink. Then he removed her stockings, unclasping them from her garter belt and kissing her thighs. Once her legs were bare, he knelt and took one foot at a time, putting his lips to them with reverence, saying, "I kiss your feet."

Then he looked up at her and said: "You are more than first class. You are the queen, the queen of my heart. My goddess." Then rising, he embraced her; he kissed her lips and told her that he loved her. Then they both got completely naked and engaged in every imaginable posture in the sexual catalog. No one had ever made love to her like that before; and he confessed to the same.

"I wanted you to understand that," Rochelle concluded.

Towards the end of the account Laureen began to think more clearly, looking in her imagination at the motel scene as if from a distance. She was embarrassed by her storyteller's lack of shame. Evidently, the woman had no view of herself, no moral self-consciousness. At the same time she felt Rochelle's aloneness, her need to communicate her importance beyond any real understanding of relationships--whether hers and Frank's or Frank's and Laureen's--and, by implication, hers and

Neville's. Above all, however, was the reference to the money that would take them to paradise.

In the motel Rochelle spoke of the color question. Would he marry her if she divorced Neville? Would he divorce Kitty? What would be the political ramifications? Would Frank Van Dam marry a black girl?

"Why not?" he'd answered smiling. "We're the good guys." No, but seriously, as for her color, he loved the shading of her skin. He'd be proud to be married to her. And the politics? Generally, there'd be nothing wrong there. Except, that is, for his current status in the party now that they'd been demolished in the elections. If it weren't for Laureen Metcalf, he'd said. Of course, he meant her reporting, her muckraking and such. But was there, Rochelle suspected, something more in that, in those constant references to Laureen Metcalf, Laureen Metcalf, Laureen Metcalf? He seemed to hate her; but was it hate or something else? Rochelle decided that it was something else. After all, no blame attached itself to him. As far as the reporter's articles went, he looked clean throughout. So what, in a personal sense, was there to hate?

"Even so, we could always go to Massachusetts," she'd suggested. She had relatives there; her parents were born there. But Frank categorically refused. He claimed that, no, his position in the party would not suffer, even in the present circumstances. He couldn't just run away. He'd look guilty. Maybe they could relocate; but why not stay in the New York area, which would be so much simpler? Rochelle saw that there was something else, a someone else, who kept Frank in Suffolk County and from her completely. Rochelle had decided that that someone was Laureen.

Laureen considered all those mysterious emails sent, as she was sure, by Van Dam during her research and after the first article appeared. If Van Dam wanted to stay in the area, it was to eliminate bad friends and political nuisances--it was to consolidate his power in the county.

She asked what Rochelle wanted, in particular, from her.

"Nothing," said the other, standing and putting on her brown cashmere overcoat. (Varying slightly in color, how much it resembled Sonny's!) "Absolutely nothing. Only, don't think you can have him. I love him. I want him. He's mine." Her eyes menaced her rival, whose impression was that Rochelle could kill for something she wanted: if not personally then by proxy. "You see," she added, rising, "I know that he'd sent you secret information about Tom Flynn and the others. I, uh, I got into his email one day . . . ."

"Clever," said Laureen without expression. This was too perfect not to savor, if only for a few seconds. Rochelle had finished adjusting her coat.

"I have already forgiven him."

"Wisely." Laureen wanted to add something about Rochelle's cross-over to the white world, rather odd coming from someone devoted to black progress. She held her tongue.

"Thank you for having me here," Rochelle said, refitting her brown cloth toque. "I will see you tomorrow. In Belvedere. For the diary."

Laureen nodded, smiling, though that "in Belvedere" sounded more like "in Hell."

Still, that unspoken question swelled in her throat--how could she word it?--how the two of them or one of them killed both Tom and Sandra Flynn. She wanted it to shout out, Who fired the shot? From that gun lying somewhere in the bedroom. Would that only produce raised eyebrows in Rochelle, perhaps even a laugh? She bowed her head over her coffee. This is a woman, she thought, with a grandiose sense of herself.

And where would Rochelle get that fifty thousand to pay for the pages in the diary?

Realizing what she had proposed to her, Laureen felt a thrill of fear. Meet Rochelle--and of course Van Dam--at the Flynn house in Belvedere? Without protection? Offering the letters from the briefcase? Surely, they'd spend the next few hours figuring out a way to kill her. Far from using Rochelle to get Van Dam, those two could knock their heads together to get her. What was she thinking--or not thinking? It was too late to undo the invitation. There was no mumbling and stumbling and backing out now. She was doomed. Even if she made Xerox copies of the stuff. Unless, unless she could work a way to have someone there by her side. Sonny? Neville? Rodger? Anyone?

"You're so smart doing this," Rochelle said. She tied her coat with the buckle-less belt.

"The last thing any of us wants is more trouble than we've already got."

"I'll leave now," Rochelle said, moving to the stair down to the door..

"Well," Laureen rose from the table, followed, adding, "about the gun, the Smith & Wesson."

Rochelle, looking back up, raised an eyebrow.

"Fired, once."

"By Frank," Rochelle answered quickly. "In my backyard. I asked him to kill a squirrel. A nuisance. Kept me up at night, rummaging in my attic. I asked him, you know, because my husband refused to do it."

Laureen smiled. "How will I be paid?" she asked.

"You will be paid," the woman assured her. "In cash."

She noticed the curious look in Rochelle's eyes, combining self-confidence and an impulse toward a wicked sort of trickery: dandy eyes, really.

"Good."

"Do not doubt me," said the other, walking away towards the door. "At eleven."

Once Rochelle had gone, Laureen experienced a delirium of possibilities. Questions swirled in her brain, wilder and wilder, so that all she could hope for now was to remember to be in Sandra Flynn's house tomorrow at eleven a. m. She paced around, ruminating, feeling groggy and then overwhelmingly fatigued. It was now three in the afternoon. She flopped on her bed and fell asleep.

She woke again at five that evening from a horrible dream. She'd been swimming, when a current took her far out to sea. There she came near a whirlpool, closer and closer, telling herself that if she could only swim around it she would be safe. But her arms became tired, and soon she moved in towards the swirling water; and as she felt herself falling into the darkness, and calling, "Rodger! Rodger! Rodger!" She awoke, breathing hard and hearing her heart beat rapidly.

She knew she had to do something the next day. The phrase "do something" echoed several times in her head. Yes, there was something, something in works, and tomorrow was the day. Somehow she'd made progress. Even with a dull-brained concussion, she managed to get this far. This far? Tomorrow, if she showed up in Belvedere, both Frank and Rochelle would murder her! Thrills of fear quivered through her body. Think, think, she told herself: with a little luck she could have them both under arrest and locked away.

She felt the promise of possibilities, but what they were she couldn't formulate. After a night of dead ends and blind proposals--nothing in the way of clear plans--she went to bed, hoping that one of the men in her life would present himself to bail her out of a certain grave.

CHAPTER ELEVEN
Dream-Force

The telephone woke her at eight in the morning. She heard Rodger's voice, excited yet precise. He'd been up all night, thinking. He'd undergone a crisis. What about the call she was supposed to get from his lawyer? He said he decided now to speak for himself. Why did she need a gun in her hand? She told him what she learned about his afternoon with Takeesha Montaigne. He became conciliatory, confessing that he knew he'd been stupid and promising that he would find a way to mend the relationship. Please, could she understand? He'd awakened that Saturday morning last week without any sense of who he was or what he was doing. He knew he'd lost himself. He was the one who'd contacted the D. A., and it was the D. A. who'd sent over the police to escort him to Hauppauge that afternoon. He'd gotten seriously involved in the Tom Flynn case. He added that he would be entering intense counseling. With this, he needed her emotional support. Finally he asked to return to the house.

"You're the one who left," she reminded him.

"Yeah, well, then, what about it?" he asked.

"With or without your non-existent son?" she answered. How did this get to be her responsibility?

"Look, I'm sorry about that."

As for talking, he'd been meeting with the Suffolk D. A. for the past five days. He'd initially offered to consult with the County Attorney's office after Tom Flynn's death. Later that day, in the course of conversation and suddenly motivated with a spasm of guilt, he'd described the accident that killed Arthur Weisskoff ten years ago. He confessed to his part in it. He included Frank Van Dam in the outrageous business of the gas line. He'd relieved his conscience; at the same time he agreed to testify against Van Dam if the D. A. chose to prosecute. Being an elected official from the opposition, Henry Stallard, the D. A., considered the matter a definite possibility, but he would have to consult a number of people before going forward.

Finally, Rodger thanked her for being understanding. He would return to the house again this afternoon. Along with some books, he'd take his computer and a few more necessaries. Then he'd find an apartment.

"I could always stay," he offered.

She thought for a moment and then asked him if he could meet her at the Flynn house at 11 a. m.

There was a pause.

"Why?"

She told him the reason, that she was due to meet Frank Van Dam and Rochelle Davis there to discuss the deaths of its occupants. She needed support.

"Are you serious?" he asked.

"Will you?"

"No. It's dangerous. And I don't want you to do it, either."

Okay, right now he was useless.

"Go talk to your counselor," she said. "After six months, when you think you've found yourself, come back and talk to me."

But he said again: "I could always stay."

"Not unless you show up at the Flynns," she said.

"Can't do it," he said.

"Did you kill Sandra Flynn?" she blurted into the phone.

Nothing. Then he said, "I don't answer questions like that," and hung up.

So much for him. She dialed Sonny and asked him for the same favor. He replied that she had to be crazy. Why wouldn't she come over instead and have a drink with him?

Then there was Neville.

"It's wiser," he warned her, "to stay home today and rest."

"Why?"

"Because. You shouldn't go where you think you want to go."

"But why?"

"I can't say. But I believe it's for your own welfare."

"I appreciate this, Neville. Thank you."

"Consider."

After a spasm of fear, she felt free, really free: strange but also empowered. How, she couldn't formulate in words. But this was new to her. Then she saw that she must go forward, blindly if need be, and let destiny propel her. She would not be working for anyone else, not Rodger or Sandra or Tom or even Neville. Just herself. She decided to take the diary pages with her to Belvedere. Why, she couldn't say: she could tease Frank and Rochelle a while, use them in some way to create a scene; something that might lead to . . . she couldn't formulate the idea. She put the pages in her handbag and left.

Her date with Frank and Rochelle was set for eleven. She determined on going there but only after she'd seen Sandra Flynn's face one more time. This was a desperate impulse; but after the sense of direction she'd felt when Rochelle Davis left her house, she wanted to see the real face of the dead woman, if only to dispel the strangeness in her mind whenever she thought of the dream she had; to assure herself, by physical evidence, that Sandra was indeed dead. For too many days she'd let this business slide. She might've waited for her friend's body to lie in state in the funeral home, but she couldn't be certain then if the coffin wouldn't be closed.

In retrospect, nothing she'd done all week had made any sense. How many inadvertent things there were, enough to make her believe that nothing in her life had any consequence. No, not Sandra or Takeesha or Sonny or Neville or Rochelle Davis or Frank Van Dam. She was invisible, anonymous, part of the staged drama of life, and they were just one damned thing after another, with no rational connection, leading nowhere. Leading her merely to fear and self-doubt: yet, she corrected herself, with this meeting at eleven leading to definite possibility. Even if it meant her death? Maybe not. She thought, then, she might try and find out more about the nature of the crime in order to get a solid comprehension of it. Just in case Rochelle's jealousy didn't prove catalyst enough.

Keep moving, she told herself. She could feel a force carrying her forward, something larger than she, but also she: she for the first time.

She telephoned the "twins," as she called them: Lieutenants Philips and Grady, inseparable look-a-likes, both in Homicide, who were both five-ten, dark-haired, brown-eyed; they wore the same heavy tan raincoats and spoke with the same Brooklyn accent. She knew both men from previous interviews and expected them to elaborate on any new developments in Sandra's case. Unfortunately, neither of them were at work today. "Off-time," she was told. So she spoke to the desk sergeant at the 6th Precinct, who offered her nothing.

Abruptly, as if to stay in motion, she drove down to Hauppauge to see Sandra in the county morgue. A quick call to her editor, to whom she promised a nice piece on "The Flynn Deaths," prepared the way. Doubtless, some overpowering, crazy wind seemed to be bearing her along, including her in its direction. Who knew if it wasn't Neville Davis' dream-force.

Chubby-faced Chris Steiner greeted her cordially and led her to the chamber of large drawers, the repository of questionable corpses. Ever the gentleman, he held his thick hand out to indicate the way.

She walked slowly. She knew that it would be hard to look at Sandra dead, distorted, and stiffened in nothingness. She paused at the threshold, inhaling deeply. No going back. Remembering her first reaction to Tom Flynn's corpse, she feared a more hysterical response: more than nearly fainting; rather, breaking down, weeping, collapsing in grief and terror on the county morgue floor. She forced herself to move toward the place where Steiner stood, like a maître d', ready to offer her the best view in the house. If that pudge can do it, she told herself, so can I.

Now came the body, head first, gliding along with metallic precision. Halfway out, it stopped. Laureen glanced down. Face upward, eyes closed, Sandra lay like a grimacing manikin. The mouth had opened a bit, showing the edges of her teeth; strangely, the cheeks drew up tightly toward her ears, reminding her of the mockery Sandra made of Kitty Van Dam and her trip to Peru. A purplish splotch spread out from one ear, invading the hairline and gathering around the eye. Beyond those effects was nothing. This was not the woman Laureen knew and once loved. There was a body, and there was a hollowness. She nodded for Steiner to close the drawer.

She had to keep moving.

As he led her out, she asked him how he managed to become the Assistant Chief Medical Examiner.

"Politics," he laughed. "I knew someone." And then as if he intuited her thought, he added, "Not Van Dam, somebody else. Which is not to say, Mr. Van Dam hasn't got the rest of Forensics as his friends. As for me," he continued cheerfully, "I've got a degree in biochemistry. In college I used to work here during the summer. As with any job, you make some friends, and you learn a lot while working."

"I can imagine."

She paused, noticing a hesitancy in Steiner's facial expression. She stared at him.

He nodded. "There was something else," he whispered. She waited. "Sperm," he said, not looking at her. He nodded. "She'd just had sex with someone."

She grew hazy; she lost consciousness. She came to in Steiner's embrace, lying on the floor. Once he lifted her to her feet, she broke away. She told him she was fine.

He had her sit for a while, giving her a glass of water. Then urgently, she rose and went to the door. She thanked him and said goodbye.

"Any time, Laureen," he called after her familiarly. "Just call first. And get some rest."

She drove east on the Expressway. Under a layer of low, dark clouds, a damp warmth had come across the Island, descending on the landscape in a mood of restlessness. Bare trees, responding to the warmth, would find they could produce no more leaves; and as if in sympathy, in some part of herself, Laureen wanted to cease and desist, but only weakly. That indefinable urge pushed her forward. As another call to the precinct brought no results, she relaxed and proceeded to Sandra's place in Belvedere.

Then the fear crept in on her, and she began to shake.

Of all the damned things. She pulled off the highway and parked on a side street. She turned off the motor, and forced herself to breathe, wondering to what degree she should have serious doubts about her line of action. She sat still in the car, pausing--and then she sank. It was all useless. Frank and Rochelle. What could she make them do and say? She was on her way to nowhere. Real nowhere. But, hold on. There was Chris Steiner and his analysis of . . . of sperm. That was it, of course. With Rochelle in the room, all she had to do was bring up the relationship between Frank and Sandra--and the sperm found on her body. With this in mind, she started the car and continued on her mission.

She drove accepting the challenge, the danger. She made the effort to ignore the dull, warm weather that might touch her with despair, that might suggest that any success in discovery, any desire for satisfaction, would be without meaning--or with a cruel meaning: as Neville Davis suggested. Of course, she knew it could be painful. That's what it meant to be good. To be real. Again, she felt that certain freedom, full of strange purpose--for herself. There was no room for second thoughts; she must go forward. True, she'd lost her joy in writing, she'd lost her best friend, she'd lost her husband, but, still, she was her own woman, free. She could make something happen, make something find its way into the open and die. This would be her act, her accomplishment. Mere writing, mere thinking, mere logic were useless. She needed to participate in the essential progression of cause-and-effect that had begun a long, long time ago--beginning at one point and ending at another--even if she didn't understand the stops along the way. She needed to get Frank Van Dam and incidentally his girlfriend, Rochelle.

CHAPTER TWELVE
The Passion of the Moment

The trees of Bluff Lane formed an arch of bare, scraggled branches, below which trailed streams of yellow and brown leaves. Above, the irregular foliage of oranges and russets guided her down Castlewood Path to where she knew she must be. The Tudor house in Belvedere had the same flawless beauty, the same faux-antique grandeur as before, though the grounds were surrounded with yellow tape, unevenly draped and tacked to trees and wooden posts. She looked for a squad car. Not seeing any, she supposed the officers had driven off to grab an early lunch. Parking alongside a yellow strip advising her not to trespass, she got out and walked to the front door.

On the way she noticed that the two Japanese maples with red leaves--the one she had noticed when she paid Sandra the first visit--had shed more than half their leaves. The sight touched her deeply, as if the branches had been deliberately shaken and the trees despoiled by some evil intent; so she paused to breathe, to recapture her purpose, for the trees reminded her of Neville's warning. Then she went to the door. It was unlocked, and she entered.

Once into the living room, she looked at the fireplace with its painting of horses racing across a meadow. She glanced at the leopardskin love seats, then across the room to the bronze velour couch with the wild, green cactuses rising to the ceiling. And then nothing. In and around hung the emptiness; an old emptiness she dreaded to confront, as if made of a strange threat; no longer as she'd first experienced it, with its vague insistence of guilt and pain. Yet, she sensed, there would be pain, more pain before the day was over.

She'd been here only once, now as in a dream. How quickly the present gave way to the past; and how quickly the palpable of here and now evanesced into the flimsiness of there and then. Was this translucent, fleeting day the only real? Was a person's entire past nothing more than yesterday's headline? So that everything except the immediately-sensed existence became a floating gossamer, a subjective formulation, a fantasy influenced by irrational fears, hormonal secretions, and personal quirks--all merely passing, passing. Surely, there must be more, much more, but who could specify the what, the where? Who could hold it, comprehend it, love it--or be loved by it? Yet there was more, so much more. There had to be.

She stood, lonely, and breathing deeply, she turned and went up to the second floor to the death scene. She was stunned as she entered the bedroom. Sandra's perfect realm had become a jungle of clothes and colors. A sensation of struggle lingered about the space--swirled bed sheets, flung shoes, upset articles on the dresser, a curtain hanging awry, down and away from the window; facing which she could see the gray water in the bay through the bare trees beyond. Overcoming nausea, she moved through the catastrophe, turning from side to side, seeking a meaning. Stepping backward in disappointment, she put her foot on an object that crackled beneath her shoe. She bent to pick it up: the photograph of Sandra and her on the beach at Cape Cod. It had slipped out of its frame; it had been trampled and wrinkled. The broken frame lay some ten feet away at the foot of the bed. She stared at the photo, feeling the empty pathos of remembered beauty; then she heard the door open below.

"Hello!" a man's voice shouted. "Someone? Anyone?"

Laureen went to the head of the stairs. Her breath quickening, she peered down. She expected him, this intruder: the tangible reason for her coming. Thank you, Rochelle, she said to herself, thank you for bringing him.

The man walked to the foot of the stairs and peered up. She tensed as he said: "It's you. I thought I recognized your car." Then up the stairs he came, swiftly, two steps at a time. She backed away, knowing this was the drama she'd anticipated; feeling herself as carried along by that larger something, her unavoidable fate. Miraculously, as if to prepare her for the crisis, her cold symptoms disappeared, but the cloudiness of her concussion remained. And where was Rochelle Davis?

Once the woman appeared, the drama might move toward its climax. She might not need the briefcase papers at all. All she might need was a simple accusation. That tidbit about the sperm was the perfect catalyst.

Then she recognized him, Frank Van Dam . . . as if for the first time.

She took a long look, breathing him in with her eyes, feeling her chest tighten. He was a big fellow, and for certain he'd come to do her harm. She feared the man but only for himself. She had no fear of the wider circumstance, ironically confident, in some way, that she would survive whatever he--and his accomplice--might bring against her. She need only touch upon what Chris Steiner had told her: that is, with Rochelle in the room. That would set the sparks flying, wouldn't it?

She stared at the man.

During the past twenty years, in her mind's picture album, whenever he might wander into her thoughts, he remained adolescent: tall, slim, boyish, with a glint of fun in his gray-green eyes and an impish curve to his lips that drove the high school girls wild, but which Laureen had come to see as a characteristic touch of cruelty. Yet as she looked at him, it seemed that the old photo in her brain had faded, and here he was, fully mature: and she had never, over the years, looked so closely. After twenty years his hair had darkened from its light reddish brown, growing wavier and receding behind two scallops on either side of his widow's peak. He'd developed a profile in the traditional sense, a sweeping jawline under a strong nose, perhaps too strong over his narrow upper lip. His aspect was one of impersonal sternness, with a hint of humor in the eyes and mouth, contradicted by a subtle tightness in his face. He seemed older than thirty-seven. He might have been an actor in the days of black-and-white movies, when such a look defined masculinity; now he was just a lady-killer on the loose; and she wondered if she could see him bending to kiss Rochelle Davis' bare feet or, rather, if the reverse weren't the truer picture.

Laureen thought of herself on that night of twenty years ago. Had she been fated to suffer under Frank Van Dam what she suffered? Had she been destined to live her life point by point for what happened to her then? Were there other possibilities? A parallel universe; another Laureen in another time and place? A white Laureen? The racial situation now wasn't what it was then; it had come around a bit: so might've he, if . . . if only he weren't so damned elusive, she thought. Truth be told, she never found it easy to hate him entirely. And yet.

By now she'd backed fully into the bedroom. She had freedom of movement and could handle the man alone. But Rochelle, were was she? She could begin on her own by mentioning the sperm business: but suppose Steiner had gotten it wrong? Suppose her intuition was wrong. It would be better to have Rochelle here. It was wiser to temporize. Anyway, there was the personal issue, between just the two of them, and that needed clarification. And there was this mess.

As she backed away, he followed, standing in the doorway, staring back at her. Always well-groomed, he wore nice clothes, subdued, expensive. His overcoat was a double-breasted charcoal-black woolen weave; his suit a dark blue pinstripe; his shoes a highly-polished, gleaming black. The collar on his white shirt stood perfectly stiff, showing to advantage the neatness of his perfectly-knotted light-blue silk tie--which, rakishly, if oddly, had thin red zigzags running down it. His complexion, as always, was pale without seeming unhealthy. He was known jocularly as the Boy Wonder; but writing about him in the newspaper, she'd have the urge to refer to him as the Ambassador.

"You wanted to see me," he said.

"Weren't you coming with Rochelle Davis?" she asked.

"She'll be here in a little while," he said. "Running late." He smiled.

She realized, as she'd stared at the light-blue tie with its thin red zigzags, that in a weird way he'd been expecting this encounter for a long time--if not here then elsewhere.

Now both could read that knowledge in the other's face. But in this confrontation, she never saw that she might be totally alone, without support from anyone--anyone--for she feared that her negative feelings about him might have something positive underneath. What if he was the only man who ever truly loved her? What if, in spite of everything, she returned those feelings?

She glanced around the wrecked bedroom. "You did this, didn't you?"

Her abruptness surprised him, as, glancing about, he answered without expression.

"Yes."

"I guessed it was you," she said.

"How did you guess?" he asked. He seemed proud rather than guilty, as if he'd wanted her to know straight out.

"Just knowing you and . . . ."

"And those missing pages in the diary?"

"Well, well," she smiled.

"You're good," he said. "Very good."

She wanted to ask, "How could you?" but she was satisfied with a fixed smile.

"Should we have a drink?" he suggested suavely, gesturing to the stairs. "Before we discuss business."

She moved past him, and he descended after her; they entered the living room, and she turned to him. It was as if, now that they understood each other--now that he recognized her understanding of him--a drink was perfectly appropriate. Of course, where they'd drink--in the dead people's empty house--was nothing if not ghoulish.

"I'll have what you're having," she said, forgetting that she'd sworn off alcohol at Sonny's place. She removed her overcoat. More to come, she told herself. Though she quavered within, she held herself well, knowing she would have to see this to the end. Yes, a drink for each of them. She calmed herself and prepared to challenge him about the sperm left in Sandra Flynn. A drink would cure any hesitancy she might suffer under the effects of the concussion. But for him to confess so soon! For her to catch him with a smile!

Removing his overcoat as if he lived in the house, he came and got hers, then took both coats to the entranceway and hung them in the closet. Then, familiarly, he went to the kitchen and mixed vodka screwdrivers, bringing them back and setting them on the coffee table between the two love seats.

"This will be easier," he noted.

Laureen sat down; Frank, opposite.

"You didn't miss Tom's funeral," he said. "I saw you there."

Her face got warm, seeing that here in these love seats, sitting with drinks before the fireplace, they, even for their racial differences, might be man and wife. She smiled.

He smiled too. He laughed with two "ha's," holding up his glass.

"To the good old days," he pledged.

"Whose?" she asked, sipping her drink, "yours, mine, or ours?"

Frank smiled, revealing upper and lower teeth touching together.

Casually, she aimed an arm towards him, her palm upward. "So you killed Sandra Flynn," she stated. It surprised her to hear the words come out. She wanted to add, "After you fucked her," but she held that back. As she stared at him, the awareness of the death-situation frightened her. She feared, at the same time, that she might lose her self-possession. The concussion had dulled her; but as never before she knew who she was. And Rochelle-- damn her, where was she? Laureen had to proceed alone. She knew, too, that she'd shocked him, for he sat still, glaring at her. She knew, too, that what had knotted their lives together a long time ago was going at last to come unraveled. She added: "I knew it."

He stood up very straight. "Don't be melodramatic," he said, even though she was nothing of the kind. Turning away and walking towards the bronze velour couch, looking out the opaque Tudor windows. "Actually I was being funny. The fact is she killed herself."

"Bludgeoned herself?"

He shrugged, keeping his back to her.

"But not before . . . ."

"She gave you those notebooks," he said to the window.

She felt a rising energy. She'd seen Sandra's purple head-wound--and now his statement, grotesque, outrageous. Her voice took on a hoarse, insistence whisper. "Yes! She sent me those damning pages. Right before . . . . There was a something between you--you fascinated her; and vice-versa; and you, you had to beat her to get what you wanted from her: those pages!" Yet didn't Sandra did give him something else, one last time, even as she kept those pages back? Her heart struggled in her throat. But rising and walking towards him and standing behind him, she felt carried by a strength greater than herself. Holding back her heart with her hands, she spoke still in that hoarse, insistent whisper: "And that's why you murdered her! Isn't that what you needed to tell me?"

Van Dam turned and smiled at her grimly, silently.

"You came here," she spoke on without holding back, "last Friday morning, just as you came here today. You came for sex, didn't you? Sex first, business after. You two had a thing between you. A few secret get-togethers. Then she sent you away. But when the scandal hit, she flirted with you again, giving you the impression that she was there for the taking. But you still didn't know where the money was. And she was still beautiful, but she was a drinker; she was weak. And Flynn's diary, where was it? He must've hinted to you about it. Even so, you imagined you could have sex with her and get it from her. I know it's true! Sex and then the diary!"

"None of this is necessary," he said, inhaling deeply and puffing out his chest. "Okay; you're right in some vague way. This is what I came to tell you." He smiled uncertainly. Then he turned and sat on the velour couch. Putting a hand on each knee, he looked down for a while at his gleaming black shoes. Then he looked up at her, placing clasped hands behind his head and smiling again. "I'll tell you a story," he offered, "just a story. Maybe it'll satisfy you. Maybe not. It's just a story. Like you, I have a good imagination."

"I'm listening." Looking away at her drink on the coffee table, she wondered how anyone could kill another person, even accidentally. Standing there stiffly, she turned and looked down at him, dull-eyed.

"You're good," he smiled. "That's why I believe you're the best one to talk to. You might understand. Why I feel that way, I'm not sure. You've understood a lot of things all along. And I suspect that you've always had a weak spot for me. As I've had for you."

His face grew tighter, paler. He smiled softly, then began. He didn't speak of himself. He framed his story as if that was all it was, a story, an imaginary event in the intangible past. He seemed to have prepared himself carefully for his tale of chaos and death. It was engagingly coherent.

"There was a *Newsday* reporter," he began. "And then there was a politician; that's all he was, a politician; but he was a good one. He had a lot of friends, friends he'd done favors for, friends he'd managed to place in good positions. In return, they were good to him for a while--and then, for reasons of their own, they weren't. They tried to ease him out of his position. As he considered what he might do, along came this reporter, who proposed to write about a corruption scandal. All she needed was some facts, information that only an insider could supply, all about the illegal use of county funds. The result, then, was that this powerful politician stood aside and watched as his so-called friends lost their seats on the County Legislature; and, even worse, stood to be indicted for high crimes and misdemeanors. Of course, he'd helped the reporter in her articles, even as he knew his party would lose because of them. She achieved a significant triumph. And there he was, full of what you might call ambivalent feelings, when suddenly his former best friend died.

"Naturally, he paid a call on the man's wife, hoping to understand the reasons. The wife, however, in addition to being unhappy about the election's outcome, was anything but happy about this fellow's visit, this fellow who seemed to be immune to scandal. So she began to rant and rave, blaming the politician for all her unhappiness, even for the man's suicide. (Odd, isn't it--he interjected wryly--how so much hinges on other people and their misinterpretations of reality?) Words were exchanged. The politician leveled unsavory accusations at the wife, reminding her of her abnormal sexuality. (Laureen winced at the phrase.) She, in turn, slapped him with references to his friend's peculiar sexual history, something that he himself had recently uncovered, though at this moment it didn't matter since the interchange had become mean and messy.

"They were still standing in the entrance. What happened then arose from the passion of the moment. Somehow and for some reason, they kissed. And kissed. And kissed again. Passionately. Then they found themselves in her bedroom . . . and you can guess the rest. The leather briefcase there in the bedroom had a diary in it--with some pages missing. Where were they? In the garage, she said. When they'd dressed, the widow led the politician back downstairs, outside, and into the garage. It was her little joke. There were no missing pages there. Instead there was an old oar. Soon the two began to squabble again, he backing away and she holding the oar and screaming at him.

"The hysterical widow went to hit the politician. But he grabbed the oar to fend off her attack and in the scramble hit her across the side of the head. He was defending himself, while she was charging. She went down. He realized that he shouldn't have held the oar so tightly or swung it so quickly. But he was caught up in that ugly, passionate moment. Calming himself, he tried to lift her up; but as soon as she was on her feet, she ran for the house. He found her upstairs in her bedroom, where she began to throw things at him: clothes and even dresser drawers. As she became wilder and wilder, she grabbed at her curtains and then slipped on her carpet, perhaps a plastic wrapper there or maybe it was a picture frame, and banged her head against a nightstand. When he went to help her, he saw that she looked strange. He became concerned. He called the police from her cell phone, saying that he'd heard a lot of noise near the Tudor house, and maybe they should check it out. They did and found her dead."

Appalled that he could relate his crime so neatly, as if it were committed by someone else, she backed up and sat down on the arm of a love seat and remained still for a moment, trying not to become hysterical. The story was improbable enough to be true. Certainly, he'd come to Sandra that day to get at that diary--come as if casually, to consummate an old flirtation that ended too abruptly. With a woman mentally unstable. A smooth, profitable encounter that he could bring off easily in this world of flexible alternatives, now that her husband was dead. Crazy Sandra was still a beauty, and she still had that diary in the leather briefcase. And then there was the fact of someone's sperm found on the body. Redirecting her thoughts, she focused, then, on one detail.

"What happened to the oar?" she asked.

He'd sawed it up and burnt in his fireplace.

"Strange," he said abstractedly. "But it was all in the passion of the moment. It was all accidental. Is that so hard to believe?"

Right, the passion of the moment. But passions don't burst from nowhere. What passion never had a depth of emotional fixations and evolved longings? What act ever stood alone? He'd come that day to the Tudor house not simply to talk about Tom's death, not simply to seduce Sandra, not simply to get revenge for Tom's betrayal, but also to get those fifteen pages in the diary and get his hands on seventeen million dollars . . . that he had stolen. And to keep himself out of prison.

Laureen stood and walked further from him, standing now by the black-lacquered mantle. She glanced up at the painting of the two horses, racing each other neck and neck across a green meadow.

Could she phone the police? Would they find her story credible? But now there was no oar and no diary, except for what Sandra had sent her in the mail. Even so, without the diary, all the cops had to do was check him out--of course, the sperm had to be his. He'd overlooked this possibility, that a lab report would nail him.

He'd lost control in the passion of the moment, and he was doomed.

She realized that all she had to do now was point a finger. She didn't need a rock, but still she needed a way out without incident. The rest now was mere unraveling--and a clearing up of loose ends--and a quick exit. But how, if it involved the exchange of fifty thousand dollars and fifteen pages of damning diary notes? It might be wise in their eyes to kill her all the same.

CHAPTER THIRTEEN
Blue Flamingo

"Tom was a good man, once," he mused. "How were we to know that he was weak?" He smiled by pressing his lips together. "From the first you had the sneaking suspicion," he insinuated, "that I might have been his murderer. Isn't that true?"

Laureen shrugged. She sipped her screwdriver, then placed the glass on the mantle. She looked down at the fireplace, then glanced up at him. How suave, how sure he felt. But doomed.

He hadn't realized that one thing.

All she had to do was get her coat and walk out. But not yet. There was more to learn.

"I heard that he knew where the money was and you didn't," she said.

"That's absolutely true." He smiled. "I never knew where the money was. Tom did. Why would I kill him?"

"For a tough guy," she smiled back, "you are subtle." She looked away. "Perfectly elusive."

"You're the elusive one," he wagged a finger at her, "You've avoided me for twenty years. We've been in the mix together, but you know what I mean."

She lifted an eyebrow.

"*I* avoided *you*?"

"Oh, we never forget, do we?" He looked away and sighed dramatically. "Still, still on that." He turned and came towards her. "Don't you understand that once isn't forever?"

"Once *is* forever," she said.

He gestured for her to sit in a love seat. He sat opposite her.

"It was only by chance," he said, "that I happened to contact Rochelle Davis yesterday. " He leaned toward her over the coffee table. "I was glad that you offered me those missing pages from the diary. For a price, of course. I knew you'd visited her after the funeral. Who else would Sandra give them to? Well, here you are."

He smiled, with the eerie, close-lipped smile of a Hindu statue.

"Rochelle said she'd come at noon," he added. "She had to do some banking."

At noon? (Still, doomed.)

And still on her.

There he was, trying to talk his way around the irredeemable past. These days his adolescent offense would be called date-rape. But it wasn't that so much as what didn't happen afterwards. And now the man was a murderer. As he admitted. And now he wanted her . . . for money. And without knowing it, he was doomed. She marveled that she could've felt anything but repulsion for him--that she did not consciously want him dead. Queerly, she began to sense an old feeling for him push up in her chest. No, not that, she told herself. But it was there, and it was rising up in her.

"Anyway," he began on another tack, "however you see me, you see me as I am because of your betrayal. You betrayed me. I loved you. I made a mistake. One mistake. You couldn't forgive me? Too hurt? I can't accept that. I couldn't . . . accept that. I was never the same after I realized that we . . . that we would never be together. So after that rejection, what did I have to lose? I was smart, daring, political. I was the man you see before you. I had nothing to lose, and so I took chances. You weren't for me: why shouldn't I be for myself. You understand? I've done things I shouldn't have. Big things, I suppose. In other ways I've done some good. If I could redeem . . . ."

He continued, but she couldn't remember what he said. She rose, went to the mantle, and picked up her glass, sipping while eying him over the rim. Clearly, Rochelle had been right, intuiting that Frank was still in love with her. Hard and shocking and scary but something she'd always suspected. But that wasn't all.

"Look at this." He signaled to her to come and sit back down again. She did. He reached into his jacket side pocket and came up with a little faded white box. He opened it, revealing a piece of jewelry, a blue flamingo in a Lucite setting. A chain of small shells lay casually about it. He placed the open box on the coffee table. "I bought this in our senior year. For you. I intended to give it to you at the Prom. A small thing. Silly, I suppose." He shrugged, speaking ironically from the side of his mouth. "But, as fate would have it, we never made it to the Senior Prom." There was a fleeting melancholy roll of the eye, barely perceptible. But then, again, that smile from the slight upturn of his lip. "I left it in your mailbox that summer. When I checked on it a few days later, I saw that you'd put it back--knowing I'd come and check on it. It wasn't supposed to happen that way."

Laureen shook her head slowly. She remembered how sexy she thought he was. And yet, she noted, he'd gotten more masculine, more engaging as he matured. If she could've overcome . . . herself . . . and they had gone on . . . together, good god, what would her life have been! Now that feeling for him was definitely there; she felt it again after such a long time. No, she told herself, don't be stupid. You can't save him. Just save yourself.

"I've kept it all these years," he explained. "I'd always hoped . . . well, you know."

She was flattered to be remembered even by the boy she'd come to ignore, to hate, almost; but this moment seemed wrong in all ways: wrong place, wrong time, wrong timing, wrong man, wrong woman--and this week after all the allusions to flamingos--idiotically wrong gift. It was awkward, intrusive. It was weirdly comical, too, seductive as it might be. At this moment she thought of Rodger and felt again the pang of his betrayal and the emptiness of her marriage. How might it be if, she wondered, though she couldn't complete the idea. What were the possibilities? What if, after all, she didn't have to hold herself off . . . so much? And then she thought of Tom and the pages of his diary in her handbag.

"I knew," he went on, sensing her thoughts, "after a while . . . between us . . . that it wasn't . . . nice . . . that there might've been some other way . . . to see each other . . . seriously. I needed another chance. Everyone needs the right chance."

She heard a little catch in his voice.

"Why have you made my life bitter?" he asked.

She heard an old emotion under the question. She wondered how he could carry a torch for so long--how he could, for all her twenty years of ignoring him, think of her without anger. This, it seemed, was the pain he needed to make his life meaningful. And then: how dare he claim that *she* made *his* life bitter?

"You were never the right chance," she answered, not looking at him.

"You were the one," he spoke, fixing his eyes on her, smiling wistfully: "When I think of you, when I see you, my heart relaxes, my mind clears, I breathe more easily. Always." He turned away from her to face the windows. "I know I'm calm on the surface. But, ordinarily, I live in a whirlwind, never resting, always scheming, always eager to win. I could go off to Brazil or somewhere far away from this political mess; but that would be part of the wildness."

"You could go off to Brazil? Or is it Massachusetts? With Mrs. Davis?"

"Good," he said, nodding and smiling, "you're good."

"She told me you bowed and kissed her naked feet."

"Really," he smiled, rubbing his chin. "Titillating, huh?"

"Doing it," she said, "must've been . . . ." It was then that she realized what she saw when she studied Rochelle's face, those high cheekbones and arched eyebrows: Rochelle was her substitute, her larger-than-life stand-in for what Frank couldn't have in her, Laureen. But he, she'd heard, had lots of sex with lots of women. Maybe that was why he never gave his sex with Sandra, and what he'd left behind, a second thought.

The man bent over and pulled the little white box back two inches on the coffee table. "When you go black, you never go back," he said, looking up to her with that Hindu smile. It was not funny. Then he picked up the blue flamingo, dangling it in the air between them. "I bought it on a trip to Fort Lauderdale over Spring Break. As a way to say I loved you. But then we had that night, and I got confused: and what was I, not yet eighteen? So you snubbed me all summer. In the fall I went away to school. I thought of coming home and handing it to you with a note. But that seemed . . . I mean, after you returned it that summer in the mailbox . . . I don't know . . . you'd gotten so elusive . . . so hard to contact."

"So invisible," she said.

"Rochelle . . ." he added, shrugging, but didn't finish the thought.

Time to change the subject.

"Okay, now tell me about Arthur Weisskoff." She was on her own territory with that. Yet she had no idea of what to do with the information, however damning, once she heard it. If she went around claiming that Van Dam had confessed to this also, even given Rodger's accusation, she'd be taken for a psycho. Still, she wanted the satisfaction.

With a puzzled look, he said slowly: "Why? Your husband seems to know a lot about him. Ask Rodger." He was up again, moving around the room, gesturing as he spoke.

"Right," she said impatiently. "Tell me how he died."

"You know that, too." His arm extended straight out towards her, palm upward. "You reported the story in *Newsday*."

"You mean," she pursued, "that the only ones involved in that maritime fiasco were Tom Flynn, Rodger Metcalf, and Arthur Weisskoff?"

He smiled. "You want to know whose idea was it to cut his gas line?" he laughed. "A question not to be asked, as you already seem to know the answer."

"I guess it was the Boy Wonder who had all the answers," she smiled. Horrible, that oblique confession, it came as no surprise: her husband had hinted at it. Slightly dizzy, she bowed her head and inhaled deeply.

He watched her: and again that sick, melancholy glance. "Not all, not all." He paused. When he spoke again, an accusation came at her: "What were you doing with Sandra Flynn when she was Sandra Weisskoff?" He spoke slowly, looking up at her as his eyes challenged her for the truth. He gestured with outspread arms in a kind of shrug. "About twelve years ago, wasn't it?" Was this his excuse for having sex with and then murdering the woman? His excuse for every bad thing he ever did?

She turned her head, looking toward the fireplace.

"You know how hard it was for me to find out about that?" he said in a kind of sneering sing-song. "The truth all along was that you hated me, I mean, that is, men. You hated white men. I just happened to be one of the entire race."

"Who's being melodramatic now?" she said softly: "Nobody's to blame but you." Suddenly compelled to get away from him--she'd heard enough, and it was time to go, that is, if she could go--she rose and went into the entranceway for her overcoat. The house was empty, just Van Dam and her. No buffer. No catalytic intruder. But she couldn't leave. She felt an opposite pull. How hard it was to escape the man: doomed and all. For his part, he wasn't going to let her leave easily. But there was still the question of Tom, the question of suicide. Pausing to consider whether or not she'd been too hasty, she held the coat tentatively in her hands.

"Oh, right," he called after her and then moved swiftly out of the living room and past her to lean with his back against the door, blocking her exit. "After all, you married a man; you married Rodger Metcalf." His smile was pure sarcasm.

"Married for nearly ten years," she noted.

"Until you kicked him out," he said.

"He . . . left . . . me. He left me," she repeated. The admission may have hurt, but she refused to allow him to call her a man-hater. She walked back into the living room, tossing her coat on the love seat, and stood by the fireplace, her hand resting on the mantle close to the porcelain pieces of two clowns.

There was the possibility that he carried a gun. She thought of Neville's black Smith & Wesson, now in her bedroom, in her dresser drawer. Would he confess more to her and then shoot her with something else Rochelle might have appropriated for him? Had he come with a gun to force her to give him the missing pages of the diary? Is that why Rochelle was supposed to come late? It was possible but not probable, she noted, telling herself, at all costs, to calm down and focus. It was still daylight. His car was parked out front where anyone could see it. But the same was true when he killed Sandra. So she kept her eye, one way or another, on his hands. Or would it be Rochelle coming, not with money, but with a gun to shoot her?

"Oh, sorry," he said, having followed her in a leisurely way back into the living room and sitting down again on the bronze velour couch. Gazing up at the ceiling, he clasped his hands behind his head. "Strange guy, your Rodger. Do you know what he's doing right at this minute? He's confessing. Not to the murder of Tom or Sandra Flynn. He's confessing to the accidental death of Uncle Arthur." He let that register. "Ten years ago. He's lost it. Brain melt-down."

"You know all this," she said tonelessly.

"I found out. Even had to go to the Sixth Precinct and talk to the sergeant there. I thought I saw you there that day."

"I see." So that's what he was doing there, gesticulating energetically in the side room. Guilty bastard. She crossed her arms, looking up again at the painting of the two horses racing across a meadow. "It does seem crazy, doesn't it? What's the worst that could happen?"

"He could be charged. With what I can't say. Maybe Second Degree Manslaughter? But I wouldn't worry. They like guys who talk and talk and talk."

She stared at him, half appreciating his smug facade: as if only surfaces mattered.

"Did you know that Tom owned a gun?" he called from his seat across the room.

"A .22 silver Luger." She was barely audible.

"Actually, Tom didn't own it. It was part of his wife's legacy from her uncle, the deceased Arthur Weisskoff. And today by coincidence--." He stood and started to feel himself inside his blue pinstriped suit jacket. Then, as if it were part of a magic trick, he produced the pistol from a holster strapped inside his jacket: a silver weapon, simply and beautifully designed. Laureen stared at it as he strode forward, to lay it on the coffee table next to the chain of shells entangling the blue flamingo. "A rare German Luger, .22-caliber. Silver in color, as you can see: some kind of nickel and platinum alloy. Light, easy to carry, easy to shoot. Of course, it's meant for target practice mainly. You could shoot a bird or a squirrel with it. You could shoot a man, but ordinarily you'd only wound him. Only if you held it this close under his skull"--here he indicated with his finger behind his ear--"might you succeed in killing him."

She stared at the silver weapon on the coffee table. Her hand began to shake. She finished off her drink, and firmly as possible placed the glass on the coffee table. No, he wouldn't shoot her, not as that blue flamingo lay on the coffee table; not while he thought she had those missing pages.

"You wonder what I'm doing with that thing. Nothing, really. Just morbid fascination. I never owned a gun. I needed to get a good look at this one, that's all. As I said, I'm pretty sentimental. And, yes, I know the guy in Forensics. I gave him his job. As it happened, I visited Hauppauge soon after you did.

She wanted to say, "To look in on Sandra?"

But, no, he'd feel too guilty for that. Instead she asked, "And Tom?"

"Suicide. No other possibility." His eyes rolled upward under his eyelids. "I was close to Tom. You say you heard we fought about things. True. He'd started listening to the wrong people. So I started asking questions about him; I found out things, things I believe you discovered in your email. There were, however, other things, which I don't care to go into."

"About his sexuality?"

He smiled the unnerving Hindu smile. Then his eyes looked upward. "They say suicides," he speculated, turning towards the window, "suffer in the afterlife--in terrible solitude, floating in a sea of darkness, never finding rest, regretting forever what they'd done."

"And murderers?" she asked, staring straight after him.

Quickly, he stared straight back at her. "Murderers," he whispered softly and matter-of-factly, "go to Hell." Did he smile after saying that? She couldn't bring herself to look at him. She did, however, hear him say, looking away and down, as if to himself: "I've been in Hell."

It seemed to be directed at his trouble with her--but, perhaps, more deeply at his own guilt. For she had the strong sensation that Frank Van Dam hadn't actually shot Tom Flynn in the back of the head, but, rather, he'd encouraged him to commit suicide. Let's say, she said to herself, that Tom, feeling betrayed by Van Dam, determined that he should never get his hands on the money; and that with his political career over and with Van Dam threatening to expose him for his sexuality, he felt his only solution was suicide. With this, she felt a harsh burning around her heart. So, in a sense, the Boy Wonder did kill Tom, indirectly.

Quickly, with the speed of vision, she leaned forward and grabbed the pistol from the coffee table. She whirled around the love seat, then bent forward to pick up her coat, and then backed up towards the living room entrance. She stopped when she saw that he didn't follow her.

"Tell me about you and Tom," she said suddenly. "Not today. Then. Last week." This would settle it all: some confession, some confirmation of her own conjectures. This would be her satisfaction, her release.

"So you have the gun," he smiled weirdly. "You can shoot me with the same weapon that killed Tom Flynn. You've got justice in the palm of your hand." He paused. "However, that gun has no bullets in it. And any bullet that ever was in it has been taken out of Tom's skull or removed for testing in the lab."

He took a step towards her. She stood her ground.

"Tell me," she said.

"You're so smart."

 She knew she had him in some way.

"Flynn committed suicide."

Yes, but had there'd been a back-up plan. He'd gotten Davis's Smith & Wesson from Rochelle with the idea that if Flynn came out of his depression, he'd threaten to shoot him or get someone else to shoot him, somehow, somewhere--with Rochelle's connivance! Once, that is, he'd gotten the information from Flynn's diary. That business of shooting the squirrel in the Davis' backyard . . . perhaps only to see if the gun fired correctly.

He must've seen a thought-process registered in her eyes, for he moved towards her and then instantly lunged at her, reaching for the pistol. As she jerked aside, the gun fired with a "pop." Both of them hopped and skipped awkwardly as if to avoid the bullet. They stared at each other, wide-eyed.

"No, but Freddy Shelbarger, you understand, in Forensics, he told me that he tested the weapon," he said, awkwardly agitated and slightly incredulous, trying to apologize. How inadvertent he seemed. Or he was just being cagey, taking another tack. "He probably felt satisfied after firing a few shots. Maybe that was it. Maybe he thought he'd emptied the pistol but didn't count well. You see what I mean." He crouched slightly, moving a bit from side to side. She suddenly felt the pathos of his confusion. For he was doomed. She felt, moreover, a strong, strong feeling for him. As if this were the karma for some sin she'd committed . . . somewhere in another time and place.

"I'm going to leave now," she said. Her breathing was shallow.

"No," he protested, "you need to understand."

"What?" She took a step backwards.

"I brought you the blue flamingo," he said, the piece of jewelry in his hand. He breathed shallowly, too, looking up at her from under his determined eyes, "because I still loved you--because I know our lives can change, and I want things to be clean between us. Why else would I have been so frank with you?"

"You love me," she answered, breathing irregularly, "and you want things to be clean between us? That's why you were frank with me?" She barely recognized the pun on his name. "I was supposed to save you from alternatives?"

"Yes."

"Are you crazy?" she said. And then: " Frank, they found her with your sperm in her. Your, yes, your . . . ." She didn't finish. Her mouth had gone dry.

He shook his head. He had other things on his mind. Then, smiling, he crouched towards her. His head moved from side to side, though his scared eyes fixed full upon her. Then he leapt at her again. The pistol fired again, and Frank bent over, holding his stomach with both hands. He moved forward with his eyes raised to meet hers, she erect, her mouth open, her breath on hold. As if time stood still, all motion stopped, and the two stared at each other. In those gray-green eyes appeared a recognition, a fear, a deep acknowledgement of his eternal enemy. Then with a slight nod, a sense that he'd known this all along, he collapsed on the floor, curled into himself, grimacing.

"Oh god, oh god, oh god." Her finger off the trigger, she gripped the gun, afraid of dropping it; she dug the nails on her free hand into her thigh. He lay on the floor, bleeding. It was a mistake, a great wrong. Had she wanted to kill him all this time? No, she was good, and things like this shouldn't happen to her. How could she have shot him in the stomach? "Are you going to die?"

"Maybe not," he uttered. He lay on his side, gritting his teeth, one hand outstretched on the rug, one fist gripping his bloodied white shirt and pressing into his gut.

"What can I do? What can I do?" She started to panic, noticing that his blood had begun to drip onto the blue-and-red Persian carpet.

"Call 911, you stupid bitch," he managed to say between his teeth.

She had to think of where she'd placed her purse. It lay at the side of the love-seat. Her cell phone jutted out from the opening. She placed the gun on the mantelpiece, got the cell phone, and dialed.

"Yes? Are you there? I've shot a man. I don't know. He's bleeding. Yes, he's alive. He's still alive." She inhaled deeply, trying to speak clearly as she gave the address of the house. Then clicking off the phone, she stood staring at him. His eyes were closed as he curled more tightly into himself. She tried to decide if this was truly an accident or if she had shot him on a subconscious impulse. If only she hadn't gotten that concussion. She would never know, she told herself, never know. Yet the drama was over. She was strangely satisfied. What had happened had to happen. And she, she understood exactly who she was.

She noticed the little flamingo in Frank's other, outstretched hand. A blood smear obscured its blueness. She didn't give in to the urge to bend and take it from him. As she stood there, she wondered what kind of special-edition headline Joe Fallon would create out of this one. For now, too, the world would know her well. Then she remembered that she had that black Smith & Wesson in her bedroom in her dresser drawer. If her house were searched, what could she say, how could she explain?

The wounded man opened his eyes and stared. The space between him and Laureen grew hauntingly quiet. Both were transfixed by a strange sense of the other.

Then he spoke softly. "I'm going to die," he said. "Kiss me."

She knelt beside him, leaned forward and kissed him on the lips. Suddenly she heard a knocking at the door, then an opening as the door-knob clicked. Soon Rochelle Davis stood in the entrance to the living room, eyes staring, mouth agape, breathless. She glared down at Laureen and said:

"What have you done?"

"I shot him," said Laureen, still kneeling over her victim. Then she rose and backed away, as the other woman approached.

"Frank," said Rochelle, bending over, then kneeling by him. His eyes were closed. He didn't reply. She called again and again. No answer.

She turned and looked up, staring at her rival.

THE END